It Could Have Been

Have Been Great

BY SHELBEY KENDALL

ISBN (Paperback Edition): 979-8-9916341-1-3

This is for every woman that has felt like she's too much and yet,
not enough.
You deserve to know you're just right.

CHAPTER ONE

It's predictable really. Nothing ever goes entirely my way. It's always been Kate Everett against the world, and I'm determined to never let the world win.

My connecting flight is canceled. In fact, all flights out of Cheyenne are canceled. Hotels are so full that it makes Bethlehem's little situation, where they had the audacity to send a pregnant woman to a barn to birth a baby, understandable. And there is only one rental left at the Avis counter.

A ridiculous sardine can of a vehicle that undoubtedly will careen off the side of any icy road. So, naturally the keys are now heavy in my hand.

Because what else am I supposed to do? Sit idle in an airport where all the subpar food options are shut down?

Anyone that really knows me understands I will not function for more than four hours without a proper intake of espresso.

"Do you have a map?" I question the frail girl with a fantastic splattering of freckles across her nose and a pout on her face that makes me believe she'd rather be anywhere other than here. She's not alone in that. This isn't exactly where I want to be.

She looks me over, her eyes shifting up and down before they flutter upward as if she's determined that I'm quite possibly the most ridiculous woman alive, standing here in my satin stilettos about to embark on an adventure that may end with the police discovering my frozen corpse in a snowbank by morning. At least I'd look good dead.

"A map?" Her dubious tone furrows her eyebrows. Her beautiful thick eyebrows that have been spared from the tweezer disease that infected thousands of girls decades prior. We plucked our poor hairs until they were too scared to regrow, resulting in the ridiculous trend of microblading with yet another monthly appointment to restore what once was. I glance at her nametag. Genovia. Oh, this poor girl is named after a fictitious kingdom from a millennial favorite. It isn't just our eyebrows that have suffered.

"Okay, G. Can I call you G?"

She nods her head—nervously, I might add.

"A map is a piece of paper with our current whereabouts drawn upon it, usually detailed with roads that help a person navigate unknown terrain," I detail out rapidly.

She blinks her eyes, her brain slowly processing behind those gorgeous eyebrows. "Don't you have a phone?"

I shove my phone in her face, pointing at the lack of bars next to the battery that is currently red and blinking.

"Oh," she sighs.

"Oh, indeed. You'd think with our technological advancements in artificial intelligence that some of that aptitude would have been focused on methods that can actually help the average person, but it appears vanity and simulation is of greater importance than being able to utilize GPS when it's needed the most," I ramble. "So, G. I need a map. Preferably one that has a larger font that I can read. My eyes are no longer made for small print."

Genovia ducks below the counter and I hear the shuffling of things—small things, large things, paper things, and not-so-paper things. I hear her sigh...loudly. Once. Twice. And then a third time. I can't blame her. I'm a lot to handle, according to my mother.

Finally, she reappears, a shiny sheen making her fresh young skin glisten. She places a wadded-up booklet that looks very much like a map on the counter between us. Possibly outdated. But it's a map.

"Is this okay, Mrs. Everett?" she asks with a tone lacking any amusement.

"This will be sufficient, G. And it's Miss Everett. And please never, ever, for-the-love-of-all-things, ever pluck those perfect eyebrows God has blessed you with. You'll save yourself a few thousand dollars and painstakingly late nights wondering what possessed you to change something about yourself that never needed to be changed. Just, trust me. Okay, G?"

She stares at me blankly, as if the advice of the likes of me isn't as life changing as I know it could be. I'd do anything for the eyebrows I had when I was sixteen before I let a girl named Kacie rip them into two thin lines that looked more like rotated commas than eyebrows.

"Alright, G, I'm assuming you don't know where I need to go from here."

"No," she mumbles before starting to tear at the cuticles on her index finger with her teeth.

I grit my teeth before more unsolicited advice spills from my glossed lips and instead focus on the task ahead. "Very well. I can figure it out. Thanks, G. I can't promise that this..." I pause to look down at the label dangling from the car keys. "Mitsubishi Mirage won't sustain some injury tonight, if only emotional. Wish me luck!"

Genovia manages to momentarily take her hand away from her mouth to give me a small wave, but I notice the deafening silence in which she does not wish me good luck. She probably won't be surprised when the news broadcasts of my doom amidst a blizzard that reports have indicated are the worst they've seen in twenty years. But again, they stopped serving coffee here two hours ago. My circumstances didn't really give me a choice.

The parking lot is empty, except for the tiny silver car. The headlights look as if they are surprised to see me, and they aren't even illuminated yet. It's probably perfectly content to sit this snowstorm out, to stay safe amid the frozen wonderland I am about to force it into.

"It's just you and me," I say confidently, patting the small hood.

But a few minutes later, after the starter fails three times before finally roaring alive—and roaring is being generous, it definitely sounded more like a squeak—I can tell the only one confident here is me. And mine is a somewhat ignorant kind of confidence, so I'm not sure what that's really worth.

I turn the temperature all the way into the red, praying that heat will engulf the compact space quickly. I shake the bent-up, abused-from-neglect-and-not-use map out, hoping my geography skills from seventh grade will somehow rattle free from somewhere within my brain to help me determine my way home.

Home for Christmas.

Because that's where you are supposed to go for the holidays. Even though my home is more of a pristine masquerade of holiday cheer than the real kind that includes a cozy fire by a Christmas tree strung with handmade ornaments collected over the years, or gifts wrapped imperfectly because little hands had been allowed to use the good scissors and tape to produce a present they were proud of, or cookies piled high to Heaven with frosting because sticky fingers and smiles had decorated them. No, Christmas where I grew up wasn't the warm kind made with memories that made you want to go back home.

My phone beeps in the cup holder before it fades to black.

"Fantastic," I grumble, my reality beginning to shake me slightly.

But I will make the best of this situation. I'll make my way home and have quite the tale to tell in doing so. The Christmas Kate wrestled with a blizzard and won.

My mother will be irritated, frustrated by the fact that I couldn't just do the proper thing and wait out the storm in the airport.

But my dad would have laughed.

I smile at the thought, allowing the memory of his laugh to trail around the ridges of my mind and the deep richness of his amusement to inspire me forward. He always loved my determination,

5

and sometimes misplaced recklessness, that made for the best of stories.

Like the time I cut my blonde hair into a short bob, convinced that it was weighing me down from climbing the rope in gym class as quickly as the boys. They taunted me for days saying, "Rapunzel, Rapunzel, let down your long hair," before bursting into a wild fit of laughter that only revved up my resolve. I beat them all by the end of the week.

Or the time I rode an actual, real live, bucking bull at a rodeo with zero experience because my brother dared me, thinking it'd be too crazy for me to actually agree to. It wasn't.

Or the time I decided that a street race in my Mustang was a good idea. Boys could do it, so really, how hard could it be? Fortunately, only the car needed an emergency room.

These were things my mother and most of the world would agree were sheer stupidity, but my dad's lips would part into this marvelously warm smile that made all the pain of pushing through worth it. He'd laugh in the moment and for years later. When I'd talked to him last before the cancer took him, he'd said, "Katydilla, don't let anyone douse your fire. You're the brightest light I've ever seen."

I'm not sure it's true—that I'm the brightest light. But I was his brightest light and that had to amount to something. If it didn't mean anything, then it'd be admitting that what he saw in me wasn't true. And I so want it to be true.

There's a splotch on the map in my lap, alerting me to the tears that have begun to drip from my eyes and down my cheeks. I am a lot of things, but I'm not a mope. I will not sit and sulk in what I've lost, not when there is something to do to put purpose to it.

"All right, this has got to make some kind of sense," I mumble as I try to figure out the map that is unfortunately in small print, making me squint to determine the direction that my trusty steed (that is definitely more of a mouse inside, just like Cinderella's horses had been) and I need to go to make it home. From my rough calculations, it is a thirteen-hour drive without a blizzard.

And honestly, nothing makes any sense, but I put the Mitsubishi Mirage into drive, and we attempt to ride the white wave of snow. We were doing just fine for about three hours, surprisingly. Until we weren't.

"Hold on, Miranda!" I yell, and yes, I named the car Miranda, as I grip the steering wheel tightly.

The road beneath Miranda's tiny tires has become a frozen skating rink, and it seems Miranda and I have something in common: we both don't ice-skate. We slip and slide from one side to another until we plummet into the snow-packed ditch with me screaming and Miranda's engine scolding me as if it's telling me "*I told you so*".

"Don't be like my mother," I scold back. "Bitterness is not becoming!"

I put Miranda in reverse before pressing hard on the pedal.

We don't move. Except maybe forward, and while I've often told myself that two steps forward and one step back is still progress, it unfortunately doesn't apply to a situation where you only want to go backward.

"Come on," I plead, pushing hard on the pedal again. "I didn't mean it. You're not like my mother. You're the opposite of her, and that's honestly the biggest compliment I could ever give to anyone or anything."

But nothing happens.

"Fine!" I sigh in frustration at the small car that's already given up on me, just like every boyfriend I've ever had. "If you can't do it, then I will."

I fling the car door open before sinking my stilettos into the deep snow, gritting my teeth as the frost forces its way through my threadbare clothes, nipping at my flesh.

The truth is, I know I'm in quite the predicament. I haven't seen another pair of headlights along the road for at least an hour, my phone is dead because I'd left my charger in my apartment back in New York City, and now I'm stuck. Well Miranda is stuck, which means I am too.

I drop to the ground, my entire body engulfed in the cold of the snow as I use my ungloved hands, something I'd also forgotten to pack, to dig out the front tires. But soon the chattering begins. The kind that shakes your teeth and crumples your spine as you begin to freeze from the inside out.

I stand up, my extremities beginning to fade into nothing as they become numb. I scramble back into the car, and it's now I realize, out of habit of exiting a vehicle, I'd turned it off.

"Oh no!" I cry. "No! No! No!"

I turn the key, but unlike earlier when Miranda had reluctantly woken up, this time she stays asleep. Nothing is going to rouse her.

I'd made her brave a blizzard when she hadn't had the grit to brave it.

I tuck my hands into my armpits, hoping to thaw them, but even my sweat has frozen. I can't find any warmth, and my clothes are beginning to stitch themselves into me, thread by frozen thread.

I watch out the window as the snow continues to bury us alive.

And by us, I really mean me.

Because most likely, Miranda will survive. She's metal, plastic, or aluminum—whatever cheap cars are made of these days. She will drive again.

But me.

I'm flesh and bones and blood.

And no one knows where I am.

Except the young girl with the fabulous eyebrows that I'd frightened at the rental car counter.

I'm not sure she'll send any rescue team after me, but hopefully she will at least remember to never pick up a pair of tweezers and possibly change her name from Genovia to something less...pear-like.

CHAPTER TWO

I 'd drifted off into a frozen slumber, or at least I must have. I remember listening to my heartbeat grow louder but slower before the pulsing within my veins lulled me to sleep.

But then, there's a jolt stronger than espresso that makes my heart hum as if it's just been shocked by a defibrillator. A jolt that comes with the sound of crunching metal and a momentum that flings me forward toward the steering wheel, my head hitting the horn, making Miranda let out a squeak.

My eyes flicker open, and my brain begins to power up, trying to process what is happening. Did someone crash into me?

There's a slam of a car door, no, a truck door. It sounds big and powerful, unlike the vehicle I am in that would be paraded in by clowns to a circus.

I want to yell. Try to open my door. But my limbs and vocal cords have been entranced by the cold; they're under its chilling spell, which makes them useless in a dire situation like I'm currently in. You know, the kind of situation that is life or death.

I turn my head that is resting on the wheel to look out the driver's window, the view completely obscured by snow until black gloves start clearing it.

"What in the world?!" I hear the echo of a man's voice. It sounds miles away even though it's just on the other side of the glass. "Ma'am! Ma'am! Are you okay?!"

What does he want me to do? I can't shake my head, let alone try to open the car door. So, instead, I blink. In Morse code. Like a nerd thinking everyone else should know Morse code in case of emergencies. I learned it as a sophomore in high school. My boyfriend was fluent in it. He loved the ham radio. More than he loved me.

Long blink. Short blink. Pause. Long blink. Long blink. Long blink.

"I'm going to try to get to you!" he shouts.

I start to blink out *thank you*, but somewhere between the long dashes and short ones, I get distracted by a darkness that seems intriguing behind my eyelids. It feels warm and welcoming, and both of those things sound like a real Christmas, so I let myself fall into it.

Chapter Three

I 'm not in my own clothes. I don't even have to open my eyes to know that. They are thick and bulky, swallowing me whole like a pig in a blanket. Not an actual pig in a blanket, but the appetizer kind that somehow makes hot dogs a delicacy accepted by most at holiday gatherings. They also smell. The clothes, not pigs in a blanket. Not bad. Just different. Like they've been washed by a man that has never met a fabric softener.

There's a snapping sound of logs burning in a fire, and I can feel the heat from it warming my face. But then the warmth increases as I hear a man on the phone. A man I don't know. A man that dressed me in his clothes. A man that rescued me and brought me to his house. And I can't determine whether this is more of a Hallmark situation or one that will be featured on 60 Minutes in a few years.

"Mom," he sighs deeply. "All I know is she was unconscious in her car that was buried under the snow in the ditch." Pause. "No, I didn't see her tracks. I just happened to slide on ice in the exact same spot, crashing into her." Pause. "I know. I'm okay. I promise." Deep sigh. "If I wouldn't have found her, she probably would have died." Another pause. "I love you too, Mom."

Okay, well he loves his mom, so maybe serial killer isn't in his resume. Although, I'm not sure what the statistics are when it comes to serial killers and the love they have for their mothers, but at least this kind of love doesn't seem like the killer-worthy kind.

Then there's the fact that I had apparently already been almost dead, or at least on my way toward it. If he is a serial killer, why would he save me only to kill me?

It's better to believe the best in these situations. After all, *Optimism is the faith that leads to achievement. Nothing can be done without hope and confidence.* That's what Helen Keller had said and what I'd written in Sharpie on my binder in high school. Although, tonight also proved that hope and confidence can create ignorance that leads to your potential death. So, there's that.

The icicles that had formed around my voice box seem to have thawed. My throat feels somewhat normal again.

I open my eyes, taking in my surroundings and try not to shriek when I see daggers for teeth hanging on the wall above me that are secured inside the mouth of a bear. Maybe I shouldn't be so quick to relieve myself from the thought that this man could be a serial killer. He'd obviously killed a bear.

The rest of the place looked as was to be expected when there was a bear head displayed on the wall. Log walls, tribal-inspired rugs, that rustic appeal that people yearn for when their homes of skyscrapers and cloudless views begin to suffocate them in their smallness. I'm lying on a brown couch with those metal studs that follow along with the seams on the arms. A worn recliner is across from me, and I startle slightly when I see a scraggly-looking feline sleeping in it. A rugged mountain man with a cat?

At least I assume a rugged mountain man. This kind of home doesn't really match with any other kind of man I know.

"Oh, you're awake." A deep voice makes my insides twist. With what? I'm still not sure. "Can I get you something to eat?"

"I'm so sorry. I don't want you to go to any trouble. I'm usually not this useless. In fact, I'm usually quite the opposite. So useful that people find ways to dispose of me. I can make myself something, and I'm happy to pay you back for the ingredients," I ramble as I try to sit up, but my head begins to do this thing that reminds me of the merry-go-round in elementary school, and I immediately fall back to the couch.

"Whoa, whoa, whoa," says the man that I'm just now realizing does match the title of mountain man, with the kind of beard that other men envy, unruly dark hair that flops over to one side, and piercing blue eyes that look like wide-open spaces. "You've got to take it easy. The grim reaper almost claimed you."

I smile at the statement. "My mother said I'd be too much of a bother for him, and he'd actually never take me. At least, that's what she'd tell herself to believe that my dumb choices wouldn't end in death, although I'm not really sure why she ever cared about me dying."

"Is that why you were out in a blizzard in quite possibly the worst car ever for it?" he says gently as he tucks a knitted blanket around me. "Making a dumb choice to see if you could defy death?"

He smells good. I know it's cliché to say men smell like trees and dirt and cinnamon, but until someone else can come up with better words for a lumberjack of a man that smells like he lives outside in the woods and puts a pinch of cinnamon bark in his coffee...that's just going to have to be how this man is described. It's heavenly. Like God knew the exact kind of scent that could make a girl's knees wobble.

"It's a rental," I reply. "Last one they had."

He nods his head as he backs away from me. "And you didn't consider staying where you were?"

"There wasn't any coffee there," I answer honestly.

His lips twitch at this, and I can't tell whether he wants to laugh or call me unbelievable—and not the good kind of unbelievable that makes a woman pulse with gratitude all the way to her toes because someone finally saw how hard she really tries, how she's been trying her absolute hardest to become a better version of herself, and a person recognized it.

He chooses a sliver of a laugh that sounds more like a sigh of what-did-I-get-myself-into-by-saving-this-woman's-life. Which, I get. I really do. I'm not like most women I've encountered myself. I'm ridiculous, frank, and more stubborn than most care to contend with. Especially if you come between me and my coffee.

"Well, I have coffee here. Would you like a cup?"

This man is the embodiment of an angel, and not because he actually did save my life.

"Is that question even necessary? Didn't I almost die trying to find some?" My head feels woozy, but surely coffee will fix me right up. It hasn't let me down yet.

"True," he remarks with a head nod. "I'll be right back."

I watch him walk away, typical jeans and red flannel attire. Predictable. Chiseled muscles you can see through his clothes. Predictable. The way he walks with some kind of I-belong-here assurance. Predictable. And well, because he does. This is his house. But what's not predictable is the way he turns and says, "Creamer? I have vanilla, hazelnut, peppermint, and gingerbread."

What lumberjack of a man takes his coffee with creamer? The more bitter the coffee, the better. At least, that's what I'd expect Paul Bunyan to say.

I blink my eyes, trying to register. "Did you just say gingerbread?"

"Yes," he answers matter-of-factly. "'Tis the season."

"I normally don't do creamer unless it's..."

"Homemade?" he asks.

"Well, I don't make it, but I like to know where my ingredients come from. You know the whole debate about how the food industry isn't regulated and is trying to poison us slowly, and there's this coffee shop back in New York that makes syrups and creamers from scratch. They made a fantastic one last month that was pumpkin and toffee. I had dreams about that creamer. Anyway, I'm just trying to be conscious of the choices I make," I explain.

"Conscious of the choices you make? Like choosing to get into a vehicle that's not even remotely made to withstand blizzard conditions in a blizzard?" he questions.

"Well, within reason of what I determine is good for my health,"

I clarify.

"Got it. Good for your health, not your life. Well, in that case, you'd be glad to know I make all my own creamers." His eyebrows are raised, concern starting to sketch itself in deep folds across his forehead. I know this debate sounds ridiculous. That I care more about what my creamer is made of than the car I got in. In fact, he's probably wondering if there is a possibility that frostbite has nibbled at my brain cells.

"Well, in that case, I'll take gingerbread," I retort.

"Is there a name to go on this order?"

And it's at this moment that I realize we haven't even formally introduced ourselves. We've just been two strangers coexisting in a cabin somewhere in the woods. This crazy, caffeine-obsessed lady that he found almost dead in the snow, now sprawled out on his couch and this contradictory lumberjack of a man that seems to spar with words in a way that makes me feel more energized than I've felt in years.

Social media and the doom scroll have really created a dire situation when it comes to conversing with humans outside a screen. It's as if people are numb to simple verbs and adjectives that make up a conversation. I haven't had a good word joust in forever, and I am beginning to wonder if I shouldn't sharpen my tongue.

"Oh, of course, duh. It's Katherine. Katherine Everett. But you can call me Kate, or Katie, or Katydilla, or really anything but Katherine. My mother calls me Katherine, and it just sounds like I'm being reprimanded every time I hear it."

His left eyebrow arches. "Katydilla?"

"Oh, well, I was eight and became obsessed with armadillos. I don't know why. I just really loved the way they had built-on armor. I really wanted that. I was kind of rough and tumble and constantly getting hurt. My dad started calling me Katydilla, and it stuck. Kind of defined me all my life, if I'm honest. I've always acted like I've had built-on armor and can do anything."

There I go again. Revealing more than I should. My blatant honesty is something that often keeps people an arm's length away. People don't like honest. Not really. They prefer words that make them feel better about themselves in just the good ways, not the bad ones.

He nods his head. "I think I'll call you Kate, if that's okay."

"And can I get the name of my barista?" I question.

"Boone," he replies. "That's it. Just Boone."

"Boone," I repeat. Predictable. I was expecting Jack or Hank or Chuck. But Boone fits right in there. "Well, thanks for the coffee, and thanks for saving my life."

CHAPTER FOUR

There's a steaming latte in my hands, and I'm fairly confident that Boone has ruined coffee for me. There isn't a coffee shop, no matter how elevated and bougie it is, that makes a better latte than Boone. And I'd know. One year I'd decided to try every coffee shop within a ten-mile radius of my apartment. I didn't exactly succeed in trying all of them. There are thousands. I'm not the only New Yorker who exists off espresso.

"So, what's with the cat? You don't exactly strike me as a cat guy," I say before taking another glorious gulp of my gingerbread latte as I look down at the scraggly black feline snuggled up on Boone's feet.

"Dog," Boone answers simply.

I nod my head. "Yes, I think you're better suited as a dog man."

"No, the cat's name is Dog," Boone clarifies.

"What?" I cradle my coffee with my legs, freeing my hands so I can pull the knitted blanket more securely around me.

"The cat's name is Dog," he repeats.

"Why?" I question, tilting my head to the side as my eyes scrunch together.

Boone shrugs his shoulders. "It's comical when I call for Dog and a cat appears."

I feel my eyebrows raise in both surprise and concern. Concern because I'm beginning to wonder just how lonely this man is out here in the woods all by himself. Or is he lonely? I suspect he is. Nothing around the cabin looks as if a feminine touch has infected it.

In fact, not only is it lacking feminine touch but any signs of Christmas. There isn't a tree, a stocking hung by the fire, or even a Christmas card to be seen.

"So, what's up with the Scrooge vibe going on in here?" I ask, skating away from the subject of a cat named Dog.

I catch what seems to be a flicker of a memory dancing in Boone's blue eyes before he replies. "I've got gingerbread creamer. And last I checked, Scrooge didn't keep a full log burning. He only kept enough burning to warm himself. I'm warming you, aren't I?"

"Fair points," I admit. "But where's the tree? The lights? The *Oh Holy Night* spirit?"

"Maybe it's wherever you were headed for Christmas?" Boone shoots back, and I can't tell if his tone is grumpy or just deflective. In his defense, I did kind of force my way into his lack of holiday cheer. Choices were made, and with choices came consequences, which he was now partaking in whether he wanted to or not.

I roll my eyes. "Oh, there's a tree and lights for sure, but definitely no *Oh Holy Night* spirit."

"Not concerned with getting back?" he questions, taking a sip of his own latte.

"Besides the part where I almost died, having a legitimate reason for not making it home for Christmas seems like the best gift I could receive this year," I answer honestly. "The only thing I'll miss is seeing my brother and his family, but I'll make plans to see them soon."

"You *did* almost die, you know," Boone states as if my mind hasn't been replaying every single thing I did wrong leading up to the near-deadly disaster. I am an expert level overthinker, constantly assessing every word or move I make or don't make, so I don't make the same mistake twice.

I laugh nervously. "I guess I would have proved my mother wrong by showing her that the grim reaper didn't think I was a bother at all."

Boone's left eyebrow raises. "You really don't like your mom, do you?"

I chug the rest of my coffee before stretching back on the couch. "Listen, Boone. My mother is not cut from the same cloth as most mothers. Her fabric is starched and prefers the dry cleaner's over being line dried. She's all sharp edges and no soft curves. I can't even remember the last time my mother hugged me or said anything to me that wasn't a carefully crafted insult. And by said, I mean by email, because my mother never calls me. So, I'm not exactly her biggest fan, but she's not mine either. She's made that abundantly clear every day of my thirty-seven years."

His eyes widen as his lips pull together in a straight line. "So, you really aren't upset you're missing Christmas?"

I shake my head. "Not at all."

"Got it," he mutters.

And then, because I'm never afraid to poke at a bear, even though maybe I should be a little more cautious because it appears he's not either, since there is one hanging up on his wall, I ask, "So, is there a woman in your life? A girlfriend? A Mrs. Paul Bunyan?"

"A Mrs. Paul Bunyan?"

I shrug my shoulders. "If you don't want people to assume you are a lumberjack, you probably should stop looking like one. I mean, really. Lumberjacks wear flannel and jeans. Usually have beards. Appear as if they've swung an axe or two. Don't get mad at the messenger. You should really take it up with whatever association lumberjacks hail from."

"Right," he mutters as he glances down at his red flannel shirt. "I just like the color red."

"I didn't say you didn't look good in it," I admit. "It's just, you kind of look the part. You got a blue ox corralled around here somewhere?"

"Afraid not," he replies, a crack of a smile finally appearing before he swallows it back down. "What about you?"

"No, I'm afraid my apartment complex doesn't allow pets of any kind. Especially giant blue oxen," I answer, allowing the right side of my mouth to curve up in an easy smile.

"I meant a boyfriend."

"Oh, one of those." I sigh as my mind pulls up a Rolodex of men that have run away from trouble as soon as they see it in me. Usually by the fourth date. Although one time, a man named Andrew was ignorant enough for six months, and I thought maybe, just maybe, someone other than my dad actually saw my light instead of my darkness. "It would be more probable for me to have a blue ox than a boyfriend."

Even under his thick beard, I can see Boone's edges soften a bit, like a stick of butter that's been sitting out on the counter for a while. "So, where exactly were you headed?"

"Sedona," I reply. "I was supposed to have a layover in Denver, but the storms grounded my flight in what felt like the middle of nowhere, which then prompted the deadly dance with a blizzard because, well, coffee. The most consistent relationship I've ever had in my life."

He nods his head. "Makes sense."

"What makes sense?" I question, looking down at my empty coffee cup.

"What you were wearing," he mutters.

"Excuse me? What do my clothes have to do with my flight plans?" And now I'm wondering where my clothes are. They'd practically embedded their threads into my flesh as they froze around my almost-corpse.

"A lot, actually," he answers even though he doesn't say a lot. In fact, he says very little. Not enough to give me any indication of what he meant.

"Well?" I prompt. "Go on."

He leans over, his elbows finding his knees. "You sure you want me to say?"

I match his movements, leaning over so there are only a few feet and Dog, the cat, between us. "I *dare* you. Be honest."

He sucks at his bottom lip before saying, "All right. First of all, stilettos? You're lucky I found you and you didn't lose your toes."

I nod my head in agreement, because I do agree. Not my best footwear moment. I wiggle my toes, which are now covered in large wool socks, to make sure they are still intact. They are. Thank goodness.

"Secondly, what kind of jeans were those that you had on? I swear they were tattooed to your skin. It took some serious gymnastics to get those things off you, and this might surprise you, but I'm not exactly the most flexible guy. Lumberjacks aren't out here in the woods pommel-horsing." He's picking up word speed, and even though I flinch mildly as embarrassment begins to engulf me, slowly thinking about how I was as lifeless as a Barbie doll as he attempted to pull off his very poetic description of skinny jeans, I'm equally as excited, because along with his word speed, he's revealing his wit, and I appreciate it.

"Then your blouse was...interesting. Very sheer for zero-degree temperatures. I mean, I've listened to you talk enough that I know you don't lack any depth of intelligence, but that thing was practically as useless as a bikini top."

"I had a coat on," I argue.

"It was cotton, which is breathable, and not exactly what you want up here. You need wool, fleece, or anything that is meant to trap your body heat and keep you warm. You were becoming a human popsicle at a very rapid rate," Boone contends. This man truly is a great sport at some word banter.

My grin is splitting my face in two, maybe not literally, but it feels as if the corners of my mouth are touching my ears.

"What's so funny? You were in the worst clothes to even attempt survival in a blizzard," Boone lectures.

"I'm just enjoying someone talking more than me. I've been told no one else can do it. That my words are kind of like the equivalent to a lumberjack's axe. Cutting everyone else down," I laugh.

And then it's there. A real smile, one that slowly crawls across his face into a full grin, and my stomach involuntarily swirls.

"I'm not so bad, you know. It's just, I didn't know if I'd be able to save you when I found you. I apologize that you're wearing my clothes, but your own were not helping with your battle against hypothermia. I honestly didn't know if you were going to make it at first. Your clothes were practically useless. I'm assuming you'd gotten out of the car?"

I nod my head and gulp, thinking about how it would feel to find someone almost dead, and you were the one that had to save them. I'm also slightly infuriated with myself that I couldn't save myself, something I've been doing for years and haven't yet failed at. But I'd failed this time. In fact, it could have been the biggest mistake of my life, since I'd almost ended it.

"I'm sorry about that." And I am. Really sorry. Sometimes the worst part about taking risks is you risk hurting others, which is why I prefer taking risks that only involve me. I just didn't know to calculate Boone into this one since, well, I didn't even know him.

"I'm just glad I found you and that you're okay," Boone says softly. He stands from his chair. "Need another cup?"

"I can get it," I say, standing up from the couch for the first time, thankful that my feet have finally found their balance.

"I'm happy to get it for you," Boone insists, reaching out for my mug that I'm just now noticing how beautiful it is. It's pottery. Terracotta colored but with flecks of something that sparkles thrown in. The glaze on it is fantastic, too. Smooth.

"This is a gorgeous mug," I comment as I turn it around in my hands. "Locally made?"

"About as local as you can get," Boone replies.

I notice his coffee cup is similar but subtly different, only adding to the artisan flair. "Don't tell me you make your coffee mugs and your coffee creamer?"

He runs his hand through his hair, pushing it back away from his face, which I can now see is slightly freckled and worn from the elements outside. "It's just a hobby."

I tilt my head, looking at the mug and then at Boone. "Well, you're very good."

"Thanks," he replies before slipping his hand beneath my own to grab the mug from me. "I'll get you another cup. Gingerbread?"

And even though he's already begun walking toward what I assume is the kitchen, my hand is still tingling as if it has just woken up from being numb. I hate that touch affects me like this, but it's something my skin isn't used to. "Yes, please."

"On it," he replies.

"Oh!" I cry out, needing my hand to do something other than think about Boone's hand. "My phone. Did you happen to grab my phone when you found me?"

"It's on my nightstand charging!" he shouts back.

"And that is?" I question loudly.

"Through the only other door inside the house," he replies just as loudly.

Right. Of course. This is a small cabin. It's not like I exactly need directions.

Chapter Five

O ne missed call and one text message, and neither one is from my mother. Both are from my brother who is currently completely distracted in his life of fatherhood, and I'm shocked he's even had the time to check on me.

I'm honestly surprised I have service, but there's a single bar on my screen. I push the missed call, redialing. The phone rings, and when my brother picks up, the most deafening scream erupts through the speaker. It's so shrill and loud that I'm positive my eardrum just packed up its drumsticks and evacuated my ear canal.

"Hey, Katydilla. Sorry 'bout that. Gracie's been teething," he calmly explains.

Kevin, my brother, is two years younger than me yet looks like my twin. Taller though, by at least twelve inches. I didn't really know what he would make of his life, but he seems to have created the family we always wished we had growing up—two parents that don't just live together but love together. There's a difference. He married a hands-on, not-afraid-of-anything woman named Maisy Jo from Oklahoma ten years ago. They now have five kids, five acres, and a milk cow. A very different life than what we grew up with, and yet every photo Maisy Jo posts on her Instagram feels like something you want to climb through and be part of. It's wholesome and real.

"Well, I sure hope you didn't get her a microphone for Christmas. Girl doesn't need to think her vocal cords need to be even more amplified, and I hate to break it to her, but she sounds a little pitchy." I laugh while still rubbing my ear.

"Yeah, we settled for a drum set," Kevin laughs. "So, are you at Mom's?"

"Not exactly," I mumble, tucking my bottom lip under my top teeth.

"What does *not exactly* mean?" he questions, alarm beginning to circle around his words.

"My flight was grounded because of the weather, and there were no flights going out, and well, I kind of took a little detour via an economy car that I named Miranda. Hit some ice, almost became a frozen corpse, but was miraculously rescued by a man named Boone that looks just like he sounds but makes the most delicious latte my tastebuds have ever rejoiced in. I'm at his cabin, snowed in. I'm not sure I'm going to make it to Mother's for Christmas."

There's another scream coming from the speaker, but it's not Gracie. "Absolutely not!"

"Absolutely not what?" I question.

"None of it." He doesn't clarify. "None of what you said."

"Kev, I'm truly snowed in. I don't have a way to make it."

"Katherine, I'm truly serious. I need you at Mom's."

"First of all, rewind, take the name Katherine out of your

mouth, tear it into a million little pieces, and never call me it again. You know how I feel about being called Katherine. Secondly, I can't be there. I don't really have a choice."

"You know I can't do Mom on my own. She'll destroy me. I need the armored power of Katydilla to take all the shots she's going to take. I'm sure she's been practicing her aim all year. Did you know she started following Maisy Jo on Instagram? Following, that's it. No comments. No likes. She's just been watching and collecting data to wield it against us."

And I get his distress. I really do. Our mother doesn't say much to either of us, but when she does choose to open her mouth, it's with the intent to destroy, like the time Kevin brought Maisy Jo home for the first time. I had to literally become a human shield as our mother sharpened her words to make Maisy Jo feel like she wasn't refined enough to belong in our family. When Maisy Jo began sawing at her Christmas steak with her knife, I picked my steak up with my hands so my mother's steely glares and pointed tongue were focused on me.

"Well, then don't go," I suggest, shrugging my shoulders that he can't see.

"I can't *not* go. You know that's not an option. Kate, you have to figure this out." His tone has grown hands and is begging.

Kevin decided years ago that it wasn't fair to his children if he decided to let the problems we have with our mother keep them away from their grandma. She didn't exactly exude warmth or even lukewarmth, but Kevin would rather them know her once a year than never know her at all. It was generous of him, and I'd promised to be there, too. It was the least I could do for my nieces and nephews.

"I'm sorry, Kev. I really am. I'll hate not seeing you, Maisy Jo, and the kids." I apologize, because that's all I've got.

He sighs in defeat. "What did Mom say when you told her?"

"I called you first. I needed to win a battle before I lost the war."

"Good luck. The kids will hate not seeing you for Christmas."

I sigh. I'll miss them, too, although maybe not the screaming from teething. I make a mental note to invest in a good pair of noise-canceling earbuds. "I'll come see you all for New Year's. Does that work?"

"Only if you bring this Boone guy who rescued you. You aren't exactly the damsel-in-distress type. You're more of a damsel doing all the distressing. In fact, this is the first time in a long time I've even heard you mention a man that wasn't a client," he teases.

"I'll see you soon." I laugh in the least amused tone I can conjure up, avoiding his request. As soon as this snow clears up, I'll be on my way, leaving Boone behind in the woods where he belongs. I'm sure he's going to be more than glad to be rid of me.

I hang up and stare at my phone for a good five minutes before dialing the next number.

The phone rings. Five times. Six. Seven. It's about to go to voicemail when...

"Oh, Katherine, I'm glad you called."

I can practically see her, sitting on her throne of a burgundy velvet chair in the formal living room that is most likely professionally decorated with so many poinsettias you'd think she owns a poinsettia farm. Her white hair pulled up tightly, stretching her thin skin until it's taut enough to showcase her latest round of Botox. Oh, she'd let her hair go natural, but that's only because white hair was currently trending.

"Are you glad?" I spout. "Because it seems like you weren't too worried about my whereabouts."

"We both know there was no need to fuss," my mother chides. "Besides, Christmas is still two days away."

"Well, I'm not sure I'm going to make it," I state flatly. "My flight was grounded due to the storms, and I rented the last car available, which proved to be an endangering endeavor as I slid on ice and into a ditch. I was basically buried alive...well, almost dead, when a man named Boone happened to crash into me. I'm at his place, some cabin-in-the-woods type situation, recovering and, well, kind of stuck. The snow keeps falling, and I don't know if I'll be able to make it to Christmas this year."

"Oh, well, I guess I need to call the caterer to let them know we'll be short one," my mother replies, as if I hadn't just almost met my Maker. As if she's barely paying any attention at all. Probably swiping another coat of that blood-rich nail polish on those daggers she keeps handy hanging from her wrists.

"Mother, did you hear the part where I almost died?"

"Well, Katherine, to be honest, I'm never sure where your stories are going. You tend to drone on into a delirious state where I'm not sure if you are being serious or being seriously sarcastic. Everything is always so dramatic with you; it's no wonder a man hasn't been able to handle you."

"Handle me?" I question, feeling my eyes bulging out of my sockets.

"You know what I mean." She sighs as if hearing from me is more of an inconvenience than a relief.

This is useless. I knew going into this phone call that it wasn't anger that was going to win. It would be her I-don't-really-care-about-you attitude that made a heated rash begin to infect the flesh wrapped around my bones and bend my knee in surrender.

"Well, Mother, I guess I'll be there if I can get there. Otherwise, Merry Christmas," I huff into the phone.

"Merry Christmas, Katherine. Tell Boone, whoever that is, Merry Christmas, too."

Then the call ends. Of course, she would offer politeness instead of concern and compassion. It was her way.

"Ugh!" I grunt before stomping my feet to release the tension that has been slowly strangling every muscle in my body.

"Everything okay?" Boone's voice is a gentle relief after hearing my mother's, like a soothing balm after having a knife plunged into you.

"Yeah," I mutter. "My mother says Merry Christmas."

"Oh, well that's nice of her," he replies while extending a fresh cup of coffee.

I roll my eyes and take the mug from him, inhaling the aroma that even makes my nostril hair perk up with excitement. Not that I have an obscene amount of nostril hair. I have the appropriate amount that is deemed acceptable. Although I've watched my best friend, Laura, have her nostrils waxed. I didn't even know it was a thing. When I'd told her that nostril hair serves a function, she'd rolled her eyes at me, going on about how unsightly it was. I hadn't been brave enough to vanquish the hairs that facilitate proper air filtering, allowing my air to be cleaned thoroughly and naturally. I'd rather have a few nose hairs than be more susceptible to respiratory infections, but apparently, Laura didn't care about respiratory infections enough. Waxed nostril hairs were sexier, she'd said. Although, I sure hope men aren't looking up my nostrils.

"If you keep me in coffee, I may never leave," I tease.

"If it keeps snowing like this, we're going to eventually run out of coffee at the rate you consume it."

I raise my mug. "You do not want to know who I am without caffeine."

"Someone that makes irrational decisions? I've already met her."

"Whew. I'm afraid I may have met my match in the honesty department. You remind me of my dad. I always knew who I was with him, and he always accepted me for the whole of me, instead of just the parts that seemed pretty."

"You said *was*?" Boone questions.

"Lost him to cancer nineteen years ago," I reply before taking a long sip of my fourth cup of coffee.

"I'm sorry." His tone is genuine.

"I am, too, but I'm not sorry I got to be loved by him."

And that is a truth I'd never shy away from. Yes, I'd lost my dad, and it had carved out a hole in my heart that had made its beating a little irregular ever since, but I'd learned the new rhythm of it. It didn't keep me from living; I just lived differently because I had been loved by a wonderful father.

I could live without him, but I tried to live better now because of him. I still wanted to make him proud. I wanted to forever be his Katydilla.

"I lost someone special, too," Boone murmurs quietly.

I perk up at this, not because I want other people to experience loss like I did, but because this feels like a moment Boone is going to peel back something important to him, and I appreciate people when they are raw and real.

"I was married once. She died five years ago," he reveals with a soft glow in his blue eyes. "I moved here afterward. She didn't like the idea of living up in a cabin away from people."

"I'm sorry, Boone. How long were you married?" I ask.

The way sadness pulls his lips into a smile gives me the impression that he's learned how to braid grief into his life in a way that holds meaning, like I have with my dad.

"Three years," he answers. "It was a car accident, actually."

My gut radiates with heat as if I already know the rest of this story. Trepidation trickles down my spine in anticipation if he'll confirm my suspicions. That she died at Christmastime, in a blizzard. I'm not sure I can press for the details since, well, look at me...I almost died in a blizzard at Christmastime, and here I am standing in this man's cabin instead of his wife.

But I don't have to press.

"You want to know that it was at Christmas, don't you?" His

question is quiet and more of a musing.

I nod my head.

"It was a blizzard at Christmas. Not quite as bad of a blizzard as this one, but bad enough. Becca never was the careful type when it came to most things. Finding you was a lot like how I found her. I've just been processing the whole situation. I'm sorry if I made you think I was some miserable ole miser up here in the mountains all alone. I just haven't had a reason to really do Christmas the way Becca used to love it," he answers.

"You don't need to apologize to me. I'm the one who should be apologizing," I say while placing my hand on his arm. "I'm so, so sorry, Boone. My ridiculous stubbornness kind of wrecked your solitude up here, not to mention the fact that I caused a traumatic flashback. That couldn't have been easy."

Boone shrugs his shoulders, and that's when I realize my hand is lingering, and I quickly retract it, running my fingers through my hair, hoping he didn't notice. "Life isn't supposed to be easy, but yes, it did feel a little like Groundhog Day. I'm just thankful this time was different and you're okay. It could have been much worse. Now, are you hungry? I threw some things in a pot, and I'm calling it soup."

I couldn't remember the last time I'd consumed anything but coffee. "If you are half as good at making soup as you are at making coffee, I'm sure it'll be delicious."

Boone lets out a breath of a laugh.

CHAPTER SIX

A nd now I know why Boone laughed.

It's edible, at best.

So, he isn't perfect...not that anybody really is, but I had begun to wonder. There aren't many things to look at in this small space we are stuck in, and I'd found myself staring a little too often, sketching his details into the ridges of my mind. He isn't just good looking. He is exactly the kind of rugged gorgeous that would sell out a Cabela's if he was wearing or using it. I mean, I kind of feel like taking up fishing or hiking or even hunting, and I hate all those things.

Any woman with any common sense would assess her current circumstances and take a chance on a swoony Christmas romance. I mean, movies are made of women stuck in similar predicaments like I am. But I'm not common, therefore my senses are directing me in the opposite direction that doesn't include rejection. I've had enough of those. Honestly, I should probably try to strike up a fancy with Dog because I've already decided that I'll grow into an elegant spinster with multiple cats, showing up at family gatherings as the quirky aunt, slipping envelopes of spending cash behind my brother's back to my nieces and nephews so he can't argue that it is too much. I've become fond of this story I've written for myself.

"What exactly did you put in this?" I ask between slurps.

"I'm not really sure. There was some broth, some chicken, some spinach that looked a little more wilted than it should have been, some beans, and some flimsy celery." He details out the list that, honestly, should have tasted better than this.

"Well, it's something," I mumble.

"Something horrible. You can say it." He smiles with his eyes, allowing them to fold into his wrinkles, which I suspect are a combination of joy and grief.

"It's a free meal. I'm not going to complain."

"You know, all free things aren't good things. In fact, sometimes free should be questioned the most." Boone dips his spoon back into the liquid that is tinted a strange yellow-green that doesn't look quite right.

"That's a good point, but I'm not sure the chef warrants a complaint after all the trouble I've already put him through today," I answer, holding back a grimace as I take another sip.

"Actually, two days," he states.

I feel my eyes widen. "What day is it?"

"December twenty-third," he answers. "I found you yesterday afternoon. I had to keep checking on you through the night to make sure it was just the chill wearing off and not something worse."

My mother had said two days on the phone, but I hadn't calculated it quick enough. Not between the nonchalant way she'd acted like it didn't matter if her own daughter made it home for Christmas or not, and the way she hadn't even been concerned that I'd almost died and was now at some random guy's house in the middle of the woods. My own mother doesn't care if I spend the holidays with a serial killer. Not that Boone is. But how would my mother know that? Moms should be suspicious when their daughter is at an unknown man's house.

"Oh," I sigh. "So, how snowed in are we?"

"Very."

" L i k e you're-going-to-have-to-spend-Christmas-Eve-with-someone-other-than-yourself kind of snowed in?" I question, finally claiming defeat and putting my spoon down in my bowl. I'm not sure my stomach can take whatever not-so-magical ingredients are in this soup. It's like an off-brand soup can had a baby with the produce they took to the back to be disposed of instead of consumed.

"Looks like it," Boone confirms before also admitting to his own defeat. Our bowls are half empty. Or half full. It seems like the entire world is always reminding you that you are defined by whether you look at a situation as half full or half empty. I'm usually a half-full girl, but my gut-brain connection has been infected by whatever was in the soup. Our bowls are definitely half empty.

"Are you okay with that?" I question.

"Do I really have a choice?" He stands up from the small kitchen table that only has two wooden chairs, in which Goldilocks would have been severely disappointed if she'd come across this cabin. Both chairs are hard. Or at least, mine is, and I suspect his to be the same.

I hand my bowl to him, a look of pity pulling down at the skin on my face. "I tried to finish. I promise. Please forgive me. It got a little better sometimes, and then it sat on my tongue too long, and it would turn into something that kind of resembled the rubber from a tire. Well, what I imagine rubber from a tire would taste like. Then the next bite seemed to curdle before I could swallow it. And then..."

"I get it, I get it," Boone interrupts. "I didn't finish mine, either. I'm not offended."

"How mad would you be if I took over the kitchen tomorrow?" I ask.

I'm scared to look inside the fridge and the cupboards, but surely, I could patchwork some kind of Christmas Eve meal that was palatable. Enjoyable even. My cooking skills aren't expert level, but I'd challenged myself for a year to cook every single meal I had, and just like anything I made a challenge, I'd conquered it with no mercy or room for grace. I hadn't slipped up once.

My friends hated me that year. I refused to go out, but eventually they just began showing up at my apartment for dinner, knowing whatever I was cooking was just as good as what they'd order elsewhere. And it was free.

I got the company. They got the food. It was a win-win situation.

"I'd be the same level of mad I am that you didn't eat your soup," he answers.

"You really don't care that I didn't like it?" I question.

"I'd be more concerned if you did." He laughs while rinsing the bowls out in the small kitchen sink.

"Do you mind if I peruse the kitchen and get a feel for what I'm going to be working with?" I stand up, and the wooden chair shrieks on the tile floor as if I've just dragged my nails across a chalkboard. I wince.

I watch from behind as his shoulder muscles pull up into a shrug. "My mom tries to keep me in food up here. I'm not sure that you'll find what you're used to."

"Does she live close by?" I ask, curious about the mother he said he loved on the phone.

"She lives in town. It's about forty-five minutes away," he answers while squirting some clear dish soap into the sink. I note the lack of blue dye in the soap. This man cares about what things are made of.

"See her a lot?" I ask as I walk over to the fridge and open it. It resembles a grocery store that has been ransacked by crazy people reeling off the fear of being told the world is ending, except for the coffee creamers. There are plenty of those, hinting at the fact that I'm probably not the only one in the room surviving off coffee.

"A couple times a week," he answers.

I shut the fridge. "And how bad is that snowstorm exactly?"

At this question, he marches over, grabs my hand, making it tingle again without my permission. Then, he pulls. Hard. Dragging me behind him like I'm some sort of sled instead of a woman.

He swings the front door open, and snow literally plummets inside to the floor. Boone has been neglecting his shoveling duties to keep me in coffee and company.

"Right," I say with gritted teeth, partly because this image really solidifies how stuck I am and partly because Jack Frost snuck in with the snow and is beginning to nibble at my earlobes.

Boone shuts the door, and the snow instantly dissolves to puddles on the wooden floor, glistening from the glow of the fire from across the room. "But what do you need?"

This time it's me that grabs his hand, pulling him behind me back to the kitchen. "Where's the pantry?"

He steps in front of me and opens a single cabinet door, revealing even fewer items than were in the fridge, but they are at least staple necessities that you can build a recipe from. Flour. Sugar. Baking Soda. A few spices and canned goods.

"If you had some eggs..." I mutter, my finger tapping against my lips as my brain begins to grab information to construct recipes that just might create us at least a partial Christmas feast.

"Give me a few minutes," he answers matter-of-factly before taking two large strides out of the kitchen. He's pulling on a large parka and his boots before I catch up to him.

"Give you a few minutes? Are you going to go lay one yourself? Because I hate to break it to you, but thinking like a chicken doesn't make you a chicken. Your body can't suddenly develop the ability to form a yolk and then build the shell around it as it exits your body. Plus, it takes twenty-four hours for a chicken to lay an egg. I need eggs right now. Plural. Not just one," I spout, my palms now pressed up against my hips.

And there's that smile again that slowly crawls out from his lips, extending until the dimples press firmly into his cheeks. The man can't lay an egg, but he sure can smile. I'll give him that.

"I'm going to the coop," he answers.

"The coop?"

"The chicken coop, where chickens live. I'm not a chicken, but I do have them," he explains, tugging a knitted stocking cap over his unruly hair that curls around the wool almost immediately, as if his hair follicles are more accustomed to him wearing a hat than not. "Also, how do you know the process in which an egg is made?"

"My nephew has detailed it out to me too many times. It's permanently engraved in my brain. I may forget how to sew a button on, the last name of my high school boyfriend that liked other girls more than me, and how to speak French after three years of classes in high school, which emboldened me to believe I could traipse across France. The French make some killer gelato and baked goods, but I'm pretty sure they invented the eye roll because they sure preferred that over helping me figure out what words to say. However, I will never forget how a chicken lays an egg."

He nods his head at me, and I feel like I just saw questions pass through his ice blue eyes, but instead he sighs. "I'll be right back."

"Wait!" I shout, and I don't know why. "Can I come?"

It's not like there is anything dangerous in this cabin. In fact, there is more danger outside of it than within it, but for some reason, it just seems safer to be with Boone than not be with him.

His eyes shift down to my feet. "I'm afraid I don't have any boots that will fit."

I glance over at the rather neatly assembled row of coats and a single pair of boots left. A monstrosity of a pair of rubber muck boots that look as if they will swallow up my entire leg as soon as I slip them on. And they do, moments later as I'm stepping into them.

"What are you doing? I'll be back in just a few minutes," he mumbles.

"Hat, please," I request, extending my hand.

A deep sigh creeps up his chest and escapes through his lips before he bends over, sorting through a small wicker basket. A fuzzy red hat is soon placed in my hand.

"Thank you." I tug the crimson cap over my head, flattening out the blowout I'd just had done that should have lasted through Christmas. Not that it is holding up well. Almost dying will do that to a good hair day.

Boone already has a black coat ready for me to slip on. An oversized coat that matches the oversized boots. I thread my arms through the large holes, and I'm sure I look absolutely ridiculous, but even my toes relax as the warmth of the heavy coat seeps through to my bones. This is the kind of coat I should have been wearing instead of my cotton-candy pink one.

CHAPTER SEVEN

"What in the world is this?!" I exclaim as I look over what Boone has called a chicken coop.

This is no chicken coop. It's fancier than that glamping trip I took three years ago with my friend, Heather, in Montana. There are nesting boxes with curtains, as if Boone cares about the privacy of all his female hen friends. String lights hang from above, and there's even a golden-framed mirror with two framed pictures of roosters beside it. Roosters! As if even the hens need to daydream about their prince charming or maybe more understood by chickens...their prince clucking.

"My chicken coop," he says flatly.

"This is not a chicken coop. I have friends in New York that live in less luxury than this," I argue while my eyes dart back and forth, trying to take in all the details. That's when I notice there are golden plaques underneath each of the nesting boxes. Henrietta. Henny Penny. Amelia Egghart. Betty. "Did you name your chickens?"

I'm pretty sure his beard is hiding his blush, because the way his teeth sink into his bottom lip indicates that he's not proud of this moment, and now I'm wondering if this is exactly why he didn't want me to come out to his chicken coop. "I mean, are they not supposed to be named?"

Then I see the name Goose. "Did you seriously name a chicken Goose so you could call a chicken something it's not, just like Dog, your cat?"

"Let's just collect the eggs."

His lack of an answer confirms that's exactly what he did. This man has a weird sense of humor. "You did! Which one is Goose?!"

He's busy putting eggs in his coat pocket and refuses to answer.

"Oh, Goose! Goosey-Goose-Goose! Where are you, girl?" I call out while patting my knees. There are at least a dozen chickens in here, maybe more. My knowledge of chickens basically ends with how an egg is made. I've always refused to pick one up no matter how many times Nathan or Jenny, my oldest nephew and niece, beg me to. I just can't get over how much they resemble tiny velociraptors, and the way they run doesn't aid their cause.

"What exactly are you doing?" He exhales as he stands up straight, proving that this coop is not a normal coop. A man of his size should not be able to stand upright in a chicken coop. That's supposed to be part of the inconvenience of being tall—having to duck. And now I wonder if there is a chicken named Duck in here, too.

"Just trying to put feathers to names," I answer. "Goose! Where are you, girl?"

"I've got six eggs. Is that enough, or do we need to encourage one of these ladies to lay another?" Boone questions, trying to tiptoe around my antics. I can feel it in the way he's holding back an eye roll to call attention to how ridiculous I am.

"Depends on if that lady is named Goose," I clatter back. "Why exactly is this coop so nice, and how many chickens do you have?"

"I have fifteen, and it's a very secure coop to protect them from predators," he replies.

"Such as?" I prod.

"Raccoons, foxes, bears. You know, things that live in the forest. Now, can we go back inside and leave the ladies to their laying?"

"Bears? Like the one on your wall? Did that bear try to get in here? Is that why it's now hanging in your house? Were you the proud protector of your hens? The rooster they'd been dreaming about since the only manly chickens they'd ever seen were hanging on their own wall?" I detail out, watching as Boone's face conjures up a new fold in his forehead with every question I ask.

"The bear head came with the cabin," he groans. "Are you done now?"

It's at this moment that Goose decides to make herself known. Not by clucking or even strutting over to me, but by spreading her wings and attacking. I swear spikes protrude from her grotesque feet as they plummet toward me.

Boone's oversized boots betray me, which is understandable. Another pair of feet could easily fit in them along with my own, and they might be feeling a little frustrated from the lack of use.

I stumble around until my feet wiggle their way out of the boots, losing any sense of balance that I possess, and flounder around frantically until my head crashes into a beam—that I believe is called a roosting board—where I startle even more chickens, causing them to join their feathery friend in flight.

Boone is quick to join me on the floor, although much more gracefully than I ended up here. "Are you okay?"

I flinch as I lift my head from the ground covered in pine shavings. There's a piercing pain coming from above my right eye and, now that I focus on it, a sticky warmth. I reach my hand up, touching the spot, and then discover my hypothesis is correct...I'm bleeding.

"Did you train her to do that?" I ask as I try to stand up, but Boone soon puts his arms under my own to lift me easily, as if I'm a pillow and not a person.

"What?"

"Goose. Is she loyal to you or something? Scared of a new hen being in the coop? I'll gladly tell her that my threat level is zero. I have no intentions of swooping in and stealing her rooster of a man. I'm not that kind of woman. I don't take what's not mine. I mean besides the eggs. I'll take those, but really what does she want with them?" I ramble.

"Well, you seem to be okay." He breathes out as he lets go of me, as if he's been holding his breath, as if he was truly concerned. "But we better get back inside and clean up that gash."

He retrieves his boots that I stumbled out of and slips them back on my feet. As he stands back up, he steps closer, putting minimal millimeters between us. He examines the injury, and I find myself holding my breath as his covers my exposed skin.

"Is it bad?" I say as I take a step back, creating a larger buffer between us.

"Nothing a few stitches won't fix," he assesses.

"Stitches?!" I cry. Stitches mean a permanent scar. They mean a forever reminder that I was a rambling klutz that had been calling for a chicken like a pet to prove a point that I hadn't devised yet just for the opportunity to be clever.

"I'm kidding," he laughs. "You'll be fine."

CHAPTER EIGHT

F ine is one word for it. Nervous is another.

Boone's face is so close to mine that I can't help but wonder what his beard would feel like against my cheek or if his lips are as soft as they appear. It's ridiculous, really.

He's just a man. I've been around plenty of men before. I've kissed them, too. I just don't really make a habit of it.

"I can really take care of this myself," I whisper, trying my best not to look into his blue eyes that I now know have a silver hue to them, something I wish I didn't know because that would mean he wouldn't have caught me staring intently at him as my own eyes had dissected the exact shades of his irises.

"Accepting help isn't failure, you know," he chides as he continues cleaning up the wound, not moving back even an inch. In fact, he feels closer.

We're sitting on the floor, in front of the fire. Dog, the cat, had stretched out on the couch, and Boone refused to move him. I'm sitting cross-legged, and it feels like Boone is draped around me with how his body is positioned as he tends to my foolish injury.

"I really need to get those cinnamon rolls started," I argue. "It's a whole process. There's lots of rolling, folding, layers, and rising. It's not something you can just whip up. It's something that takes time and, well, the clock is ticking."

"The snow hasn't even stopped falling. I don't think time is really a problem," he replies while gently biting down on the tip of his tongue as he focuses on what he is doing. It would feel hot in here right now even if there wasn't a roaring fire. "Cinnamon rolls though, huh? That sounds amazing."

I bite at the bait to distract myself as I flinch when he applies what appears to be alcohol to the gash. "I learned how to make them a few years ago. I didn't really grow up learning how to cook. In fact, I don't really remember being allowed in the kitchen. One year I was determined to figure it out. I made every single thing I ate for an entire year. Those first meals were inedible, but I swallowed them down, because not swallowing them down would've meant having to swallow my pride, and that wasn't an option."

I can't help but stare at his lips as they stretch out into a smile. "You really don't like to be proved wrong, do you? Not even by yourself."

"I don't mind being wrong; it's the part where people stay wrong instead of figuring out how to make it right. Or even refusing to acknowledge there is a way to make it right. We can always right a wrong. I just think most people don't like the effort that comes with it," I explain.

"Like cooking for an entire year until you got it right?" he questions as he pulls away from me, allowing air to finally fill my lungs.

"Exactly. Just because I got it wrong, didn't mean I had to stay wrong. I just did it repeatedly until I got it right. It didn't take the entire year, by the way. I was mastering some pretty complex dishes by month three," I reveal proudly.

I watch as he prepares a bandage before invading my personal space again and very carefully placing it over my eye. "There."

But Boone lingers, and it's in that lingering that fine really morphs into a full-fledged version of nervousness, with my palms coating themselves in sweat and everything.

I can't kiss him. It would be wrong. I don't even know him. Not really. He's just some Christmas lumberjack angel that happened to rescue me, allowing me to have a chance to live out a longer life than one that tragically ended at thirty-seven years.

He's just a man that continues to surprise me with his coffee creamer, handmade coffee mugs, fancy chicken coop, and feelings. Feelings that I'm wondering if he's having or if I'm just delirious. Which is a serious possibility between the car accident and head injury. And I'm just a woman that shouldn't kiss a man because I'm snowed in with him. He lost his wife in the same way he found me. I don't even know if he's kissed another woman since he lost her. He's vulnerable. Maybe. I think.

Kissing him doesn't really seem like it would just be kissing him. It feels like it might be knowing him and then wanting to know more.

This really doesn't have to be anything more than it is. Besides, it really doesn't make sense. Real life will resume as soon as the snow melts.

I uncross my legs and scoot away from Boone before standing up and brushing myself off. "Cinnamon rolls."

"Right. Cinnamon rolls," he repeats as he stands up almost as quickly as I did.

And I can't be sure, but it looks like he's blinking back something that makes me think I'm not the only one that was arguing with their thoughts.

CHAPTER NINE

The cabin feels darker as night creeps in. The windows have long been curtained by the unrelenting snow, but the lack of sun makes everything inside seem a little colder, and it sends a shiver up my spine that evokes a physical movement that catches Boone's attention.

"Are you okay?" He rushes over, his large hands swallowing up my upper arms from behind. The chill is suddenly doused.

"It just felt cold in here for a second," I reply way too breathlessly. "What time is it?"

"Probably time for food and not coffee," he says playfully, his hands dropping from my arms, inviting the cold back to my skin. "I can fix soup again."

"You step away from the kitchen, sir. Coffee is what you do best, so just stay in your lane," I demand.

"But I thought you said anyone can put enough effort in to right a wrong," he teases, repeating back my own words of wisdom. "You could teach me a few skills as payment for saving your life. Turn this lumberjack into a chef, or at least a man who can cook for himself. I think it's the least you could do."

Boone is beginning to melt, not that he had ever been rigid. He was softer than I expected, and I didn't really expect a lot since I hadn't exactly expected to be in his cabin for Christmas. But I could tell there was something giving way as his smiles came more easily, and he seemed...less tall.

Was that a thing? Could people shrink as you got to know them?

"I suppose." I slowly succumb to his request, telling myself this is the only thing I can succumb to.

"So, can I do something for supper while you start on the cinnamon rolls?" he asks with what seems to be a thread of enthusiasm woven through his tone.

"How many eggs did you collect?" I question.

"Six."

"Do you think the ladies have laid more?" I'm calculating what I will need for the rolls and what he'll need to make omelets.

"I can go check," he answers quickly, already rushing toward the door without me having to prompt him.

He's out the door in less than two minutes, and when the door closes, I let out the carbon dioxide that I'm trying to convince myself is slowly poisoning me with its minimum toxicity. That would help explain the flushing, the confusion, and the shortness of breath.

It's either carbon dioxide poisoning or it's Boone.

I'm not ignorant, though. It's not the carbon dioxide.

This entire thing is a bad idea. Boone's proximity is beginning to sand away at my own protective shell. I don't really want to admit it, and wouldn't admit it to him, but I have to admit it to myself, if only to keep myself from doing something utterly stupid.

I assess my surroundings. This kitchen is too small. We need some kind of island to separate us, to make sure proximity doesn't wreak havoc on our very separate, very different, very real lives.

"Three more!" Boone announces as soon as he enters back into the cabin. "Also, it's stopped snowing. Now we'll just have to wait for the trucks to come through to clear the roads."

"Oh." I exhale and then quickly attach a smile to my response. My pulse is trying to figure out whether to beat relief or disappointment. It should most definitely be relief, but sometimes the body isn't responsive to reason. "That's great. How long until that happens?"

"Hard to tell. With it being Christmas Eve tomorrow, they may try to get to it more quickly, or it may delay them," he explains while he shrugs off his coat and steps out of his boots. "You're most likely stuck with me for another day, at least."

"How was Goose?" I ask, changing the subject.

"Honestly? She looked relieved that it was just me." He walks through the doorway and shows me the three eggs as if they are prized possessions, and they kind of are. Two brown and one blue.

"Perfect," I reply. "I'm going to teach you how to make omelets. Have you made them before?"

"Made them, yes. Ate them, no," he answers.

I nod my head. "All right, well, you'll need a small onion from the cabinet, the half block of cheese from the fridge, and six eggs. Normally, I would make them with red bell peppers, some fresh garlic, crispy bacon, and my favorite gouda cheese, but we'll make this work. Promise. You'll need a cutting board, knife, bowl, whisk, small frying pan, and a spatula, if you want to gather those up."

"Got it." Then he's a blur around the kitchen, opening drawers and cabinets like he's even unsure where these basic cooking necessities are located. But finally, his movements slow, and he comes back into focus with an eager expression peeking out from behind his beard.

I grab the bowl, whisk, and three of the eggs. I begin cracking them into the bowl.

Boone's shadow is soon blocking any light from behind, and his warmth is radiating as if he's fire himself and the flames are licking at my skin. "Shouldn't I be doing this?"

"I'm going to make the first one so you can watch, and then you can make the second," I explain, trying to keep my hands steady as I crack the second egg. "Do you mind getting some milk out of the fridge?"

He takes one step over toward the fridge, retrieving the milk in seconds. "Here."

"Thanks," I reply. "I like to just put a drizzle of milk when whisking my eggs. It makes the omelet a little fluffier."

Then I go to work chopping onions, trying not to think about how Boone is watching my every movement. I know he's not judging me and that he truly wants to learn, but his gaze is incredibly intense, as if this is much more serious than making a simple omelet. As if I'm performing some kind of life-saving surgery.

I quickly have everything ready to go and turn the burner on.

"Okay, we only have butter to work with since we couldn't find any cooking oil, so we want to cook at a very low heat, which is fine because the trick with cooking an omelet is finding the perfect temperature that allows the egg to not cook too quickly while the ingredients inside of it have enough time to melt together."

"Oh," Boone sighs. He's taken to leaning up against the small kitchen wall with his arms crossed, making his muscles quite literally look as if they'll rip his flannel shirt.

"Oh?" I question as I make sure the butter coats the pan entirely.

"Yeah, I always cook everything on high. It gets done quicker, right?" he admits while he shrugs his shoulders.

"While there are a few foods that are great done quickly, the best things take a little extra time at lower heats. It makes things more tender and flavorful." I try to explain while carefully pouring my whisked eggs into the pan, hearing the soft sizzle as they hit the pan.

"Was that statement just about food or about life?" he questions.

"What?" I watch as the egg thickens enough so I can add in the onions, cheese, and spices.

"It's just the way you said it made it seem like it could be applied to things other than food." He pushes himself off the wall and takes the two short steps over to me, looking into the pan at what I'm doing.

"I guess other things in life are better when they've had a little extra time," I muse, not wanting to compare myself to a pan full of eggs, but aging could kind of be that way if you allowed it. I've been watching my friends for the last several years reject the idea of getting older, as if aging is some kind of curse and not a gift. But I am approaching the age in which my dad had died, and I want to feel what he didn't get the chance to.

Am I getting better with extra time? I sure hope so.

"It smells amazing," he comments, inhaling deeply as he stoops over my shoulder, once again invading my personal space and making carbon dioxide reside a little too long within my lungs.

I fold what appears to look like an egg tortilla in half, allowing it to fully form into what it needs to be, clearing my throat. "See how the egg isn't burnt at all on the outside? It's perfectly fluffy, expanding as the ingredients inside cook, too."

He nods his head, his breath heavy above me.

"Plate, please?" I request with my hand held out.

A chipped floral plate that has seen better days is soon heavy in my hand. I take the spatula and gently lift the omelet, sliding it effortlessly onto the dish.

"Your turn," I say, handing over the spatula.

Nerves stretch out the skin around his eyes, and his eyebrows shoot up in protest. "You're going to coach me, right?"

"Nope," I reply. "I'm going to eat my omelet over here while you make yours."

I strut over to the small kitchen table, lowering myself down to the chair with a smirk stitched on my lips.

I'm hungry, but more than that, I need fresh oxygen that isn't being shared with Boone. It's only a few feet apart, but it feels like

I'm in a different time zone with how my chest suddenly feels it has permission to rise and fall again.

"But what if I do it wrong?" he questions as he assesses all the ingredients and kitchen tools in front of him.

"But what if you do it right?" I tease. "I don't want to steal your joy in doing it right. You deserve all that joy to yourself."

I watch him carefully as I devour my omelet in less bites than I should take, but it's been a little too long since I've had decent nourishment. And unfortunately, coffee doesn't count as nourishment. Something my brother reminds me of often when he remembers to lecture me on taking care of myself.

Boone is bent over the stove, carefully poking at the omelet with his spatula, trying to determine if it's done.

I appreciate that he is sincere in his request for help when it comes to cooking. He truly does seem to want to learn, which is made even more evident when he turns off the burner, places the omelet on another chipped and fading ceramic plate, and then presents it to me on the kitchen table with a grin that practically takes up his entire face.

"Well done!" I exclaim as I give him three small claps, and I mean it; the texture and presentation of his omelet looks like a duplicate of mine.

"Taste it!" he demands with as much excitement as a kid that just discovered presents under the Christmas tree. Although, he has no tree, and I can't believe that I'm actually going to admit it to myself, but I really hate the thought of not having a Christmas tree this year, even my mother's professionally decorated one lacking any ornaments that hint at the fact that a family once lived there.

"I've already had one," I argue. "You deserve that all to yourself."

He takes his fork, cuts off a piece, and slides it over onto my plate. Then he dares to push his bottom lip out in a pout. This large man of a man is officially pouting. And it's, unfortunately, absolutely endearing.

I stab the piece of omelet that he's offered me and smile at Boone before putting it in my mouth. It melts on my tongue, making my eyelids flutter. "Boone! This is better than mine!"

"Really?" His question is strung out with a hopeful breath to it.

"Really," I answer. "Did you do anything different to it?"

"I didn't, but maybe Goose did." He cuts another piece from it and takes a bite himself, grinning in satisfaction when he realizes that it truly is amazing.

"What does Goose have to do with it?" I ask, my eyebrows furrowing. We both had the same eggs. Three of them. All from the same coop.

"I think I had one of Goose's eggs in my stash. I bet she laid it with a little extra love for me since I'm her mighty rooster and everything," he teases.

"She would," I mumble while standing up, taking my plate to the sink.

He nods his head, still grinning while basically inhaling the rest of his omelet as if it were air.

"Hey, Boone," I say, while rinsing my dishes. "Is there enough hot water for a shower, with the generator and everything?"

"Oh. Oh, yeah, but there's kind of a trick to the faucet. I can go show you," he answers, putting his plate down on the kitchen table before leaving the room and, I guess, expecting me to follow him.

Which I do.

He's already in the bathroom, grabbing a fresh towel from the cabinet for me before I catch up with him. "I've been meaning to fix it for a while, but since it's just me, I've kind of just learned the quirks of the pipes instead of fixing them."

I scoot between him and the shower, looking at what I'm working with. Looks like a totally normal bathtub-shower combination to me. Standard equipment. Nothing fancy, like my shower back at my apartment that has four shower heads surrounded by glossy white tiles from floor to ceiling, but it'll do.

"Okay, so the trick with the knob is: you have to jiggle more to the left than the right for it to trigger the hot water. If you just turn it or accidentally jostle it wrong, it'll go straight back to ice-cold water," he tries to explain.

"I'm sure I can figure it out," I say, shrugging my shoulders. It's a shower. How complicated can it be?

CHAPTER TEN

T urns out...pretty complicated.

"C'mon," I beg the hard-water-stained silver handle. "Please, just give me two minutes of hot water. That's it. That's all I need. Nothing much. That's basically a trial period. A really short one. And I'll give you a raving review. I'm great at writing those. Fantastic even. Everyone will want to shower here soon."

But the water keeps dripping cold, and yes, dripping. Boone could stand to invest in a new showerhead. I've been standing outside the shower, wrapped in the small blue towel Boone retrieved for me, for around five minutes now. The pipes are stubborn, but they aren't quite as stubborn as I am.

I jiggle the handle again, more to the left than the right just like Boone instructed.

Finally, the water warms from freezing to tepid. I'll take it.

"Thank you!" I exclaim before dropping my towel and stepping into the bathtub carefully as it groans beneath my weight. Nothing like a moaning piece of plastic to make you feel the weight of the world on your shoulders and your bones.

The water, while more frigid than I'd like, feels cleansing, and I breathe a sigh of relief, but the relief soon turns to panic as the temperature heats to a boil that feels as if it's melting my epidermis right off me. I scream, more loudly than I'd like, before I try to dodge the splattering lava to jostle the knob again, except I must jiggle it too harshly to the right because the lava quickly turns to what feels like frozen bullets tearing through my flesh.

I scream again.

And again.

And to my dismay...again.

"Kate?! Are you okay?" Boone shouts from the other side of the bathroom door.

I jiggle the knob again while yelling, "I'll be fine!"

But I'm not fine, because I jostle too hard again, and the showerhead quickly swaps to raining down fire. Before I can stop it, another scream escapes through my lips, which are still trembling from the icy water that had begun to numb me through.

"I'm coming in!" Boone announces.

"No! Don't come in!" I yell, arguing while nudging the faucet again, praying it'll finally submit to my own stubbornness. It can't win. Not today. Not like this. Not naked in a-man's-I-really-don't-know-much-about-besides-he-makes-a-fantastic-coffee-and-has-chickens's shower.

But the pipes don't give up. In fact, they seem to stand firm in their hardheadedness. So, I pull once more, but I must pull too hard because while the handle is still in my hand, it is no longer attached to the wall, and I'm stumbling backward, ramming into the back of the shower.

I hear the bathroom door slam open and Boone yell, "Kate!"

On my descent down, I reach out with my other hand for the shower curtain covered in bears and trees, trying to wrap myself in it. I need some of my dignity to stay intact.

I hear a lot of things: the thud of my body as it hits the fiberglass, the ripping of the shower curtain as it tears through the shower rings from the force of my weight, the sound of Boone's heavy footsteps as he runs toward me, and what I can only imagine is the cackling of the pipes as water continues to pour down on me...finally at a temperature that feels perfect.

Because of course.

"Kate, are you all right?" Boone is speaking, but one of his large hands is covering his eyes. "I'm not going to look until you give me the okay."

My neck is throbbing from the way it's angled against the tub, but I glance down at my body, which is thankfully completely covered. "You can look."

Boone's eyes open, quickly assessing the situation. He steps over toward the shower wall, seeing that the faucet handle is missing. "What happened?"

"I jiggled too hard," I mumble, trying to sit up but wincing as I do.

"Whoa. Easy, Kate. Let me help you," he says as he bends over me to try to scoop me up, letting the water soak through his flannel shirt.

"No! I'm fine. Don't touch me!" I exclaim. I don't want his bare hands to find my bare skin that is most likely bruised beneath this shower curtain.

He freezes at my words. "Okay, so how do you want me to help you?"

I extend the handle that I'm still holding onto and nod my head toward the water.

"Got it," he replies as he takes the handle, fitting it back over some metal part that it had broken free from. Within seconds, he manages to attach the handle and turn the water off.

"Thank you." I sigh, trying to sit up, but this time my wince turns into a whine, and Boone is soon on his knees beside me. "I'm okay."

"You are not okay," he contends. "You need to let me help you, Kate."

"I feel like all I've done is create problems with which you need to help me," I complain, because it's true. This is not like me. At all. My brother was right when he said I was usually a damsel that was doing all the distressing. I don't need help, and I sure don't get myself into situations that make me have to ask for it.

"That's not true. You've helped me, too," Boone argues. "You just helped me make an omelet."

"Really? That's the best you've got to ease my mind? A stupid omelet," I groan.

"To be fair, it was a really good omelet." Then his lips curve up in that gut-warming smile of his, and I can't help but smile back. He's also soaking wet, water dripping from his beard.

"Okay, fine. It was a really good omelet. So, how are we going to do this?" I ask.

"I can close my eyes as I pick you up?" he suggests.

"Um, no. Going in blind is not the answer," I say sternly through gritted teeth, trying to conceal the stinging pain pulsing up my spine to my neck.

"Okay, well what do you suggest?"

He's looking at me, not at my body but into my eyes, and I truly do appreciate that he is focusing there instead of anywhere else. "Do you have gloves?"

Frown lines soon dent into his face. "Of course."

"Okay, so go put those on, and I'll do my best to wiggle this shower curtain around my body. Then you can help gently lift me out of this tub, and I can assess what is hurting."

He tilts his head, and I can tell he has questions, but instead of asking them, he dutifully stands up and leaves the bathroom to retrieve gloves. Gloves that will keep him from touching my skin, because honestly, I'm not afraid of him touching me—I'm afraid of how I might feel if he does.

And what is the popular saying? Catch flights, not feelings? I'll be on a plane in just a couple days, and I don't need to have any feelings keeping me grounded.

He promptly returns with mittens on. "Ready?"

"I suppose so," I mutter.

Boone carefully slips his gloved hands under my body, which is clothed in the shower curtain that I've managed to create into a more modest dress than most girls wear to prom. Stylish, too. I mean, who wouldn't want to wear a dingy dress with bears on it?

As he lifts me slowly, I try not to wince when my head wobbles, but Boone notices.

"What's wrong?" he asks with a slight panic to his breath.

"It's my neck," I groan.

"Lean into me," he replies.

"What?" I ask, more panic to my breath than there was to his.

"Lay your head on my chest. I've got you," he clarifies.

And while I know my neck will dull in its throbbing if I do, I'm not sure my heart will do the same. But I reluctantly lean in because I'm afraid the pain in my neck will make me cry if I don't, and I'm not crying in front of this man. After all, I'm not a mope.

I feel my heart begin to pulse against my thin skin as I rest against Boone's chest and inhale the strength of him, and as I do, I swear I feel the tempo of his heart pick up its pace, too.

CHAPTER ELEVEN

"It's just a massage, Kate," Boone argues.

"I'm fine. Truly. I've been taking care of myself for years, Boone. Basically, my entire life." I cross my arms, looking down at him as he sits on the couch in front of the fire.

"It's practically medical. Just let me help you," he sighs. "This is not a big deal. What else are we going to do? Really?"

I look around the room. Boone doesn't even have a television, and there's only a small bookshelf with about twenty books on it.

"Don't you get bored up here with nothing to do?" I ask. "I mean, what *do* you do? Are you just up here hibernating like a bear, slumbering all day and all night? I'm guessing you're not a sports guy since you lack an oversized screen, and either you only read a few favorite books, or you don't read at all. Can you read?"

"I can read," Boone laughs. "And I like being bored. Nobody is bored enough anymore. Now, please just sit down so I can help you. I can see you wincing, Kate. You might be tough, but you're still human."

"What if I'm not human?" I question, tilting my head to the

side, trying to hide the fact that the slight movement feels like it might as well decapitate me.

"Well, maybe finicky water pipes are your kryptonite then," Boone teases while shaking his head. "Kate, if you don't sit down and let me help you, I'm going to stop making you coffee."

My eyes widen. "You wouldn't!"

Boone smirks. "Try me."

"You're mean," I sigh as I carefully sit down in front of him.

"Sure, because helping you is cruel," he replies.

"Holding my coffee hostage is not helping me," I argue as Boone's fingers find my skin. So much for him not touching me.

Boone doesn't reply. Instead, his thumbs begin to softly rub against my neck, causing me to flinch with pain and yet breathe a sigh of relief when he finally unties a knot beneath my flesh with his bare hands.

The air between us feels heavy and smells like peppermint, because, naturally, Boone, the lumberjack full of surprises, has a collection of herbal remedies.

"Is the pressure okay?" he questions.

"You're perfect." The words linger between us before I realize what I've said, feeling my face flush before I stutter, "I mean, it's perfect. Of course. You're not perfect. You're great, but I'm sure you've got some flaws you just haven't thought of revealing to me yet. Now would be a great time, by the way, since I seem to be revealing all of mine. I mean, you already know that I'm emotionally and physically dependent on coffee, that I ramble way too much and say things that I should probably keep locked up tight somewhere inside my brain, that I obsess over things until I master them, and well, have a hard time accepting help."

His fingers pause. "Those aren't all flaws, Kate."

"Then what else are they? They aren't exactly my best traits," I answer.

"Or maybe they are, and you've just been told they aren't," he replies, and I feel a crack in my armadillo shell, as if he's managed to see the soft part of me that I always try to protect. I am honest in a lot of ways, but I've also learned how to protect myself.

"You don't really know me," I mutter.

"Well, you don't really know me, either," he argues. "In fact, I think you assumed a lot, with me being a man that dresses in red flannel living up in the mountains by himself."

"I suppose that's true," I admit. "In my defense, I woke up in a new place with a stranger."

"In my defense, I rescued a woman that almost killed herself in a blizzard because she couldn't stay somewhere where there wasn't coffee," he jests.

"Fair point. So, let's get to know each other instead of continuing to just tiptoe around what we think we know," I suggest as I carefully untangle my legs and attempt to stand up. Boone puts his hands around my waist, helping me up.

Dog is curled up in the chair, so I turn around to sit beside Boone on the couch, pulling my legs up underneath my body. I'm wearing a pair of Boone's thermals, my hair still damp from the shower I took, if you could call it that.

"All right," Boone says before extending his hand to me. "Hi,

I'm Boone Montgomery."

My lips twist, wanting to smirk, before I put my hand in his for a handshake and say, "Kate Everett."

"Kate as in Katherine?" There's a daring spark in the way Boone is looking at me.

"Katherine if you want me to hate you all of your life," I reply, my words smooth and sharp as if they are a sword, while arching my eyebrows.

"I'd prefer you didn't," he laughs. "So, Kate, what do you do for a living?"

"I'm a marketing manager for an ad agency," I answer swiftly.

He nods his head. "Do you enjoy it?"

"Mildly. I'm good at it, but I wouldn't say I necessarily enjoy it. I enjoy the life I have from the paycheck attached to the job. What do you do for a living, Boone?"

I have been wondering what Boone actually does. Do lumber-jacks split wood for a living and sell it? Build houses? Chicken coops with luxury accommodations?

"Well, I make and sell coffee mugs. I have a shed out back that's my studio. It's not a lot, but it's something."

My brain starts processing a marketing plan that would put Boone's mugs on the map, that would cause mass sellouts and monetary success, but at the same time, I don't think Boone would want that kind of success. He seems like the kind that prefers the quiet kind of living.

"You sell those mugs?! I need to put in an order, stat. What's your turn around? Think you could teach me how to make them?

Is it hard?"

Boone's baby-blue eyes widen slightly, allowing me to see his amusement more clearly before he says, "Yes, I sell them. The entire process from throwing the clay to glazing takes two to three weeks. I'm not sure what my teaching skills are like, and it's not hard, but it's not exactly easy, either. It's an art."

"The omelet proves you are good at learning, so maybe you are good at teaching. Have you always been interested in pottery?" I question.

He shakes his head. "No. I started pottery when I moved up here after Becca died. If she knew I was a potter now, she'd call me a liar. Honestly, I needed something to work on with my hands, and I wanted to understand pottery because of the Master Potter."

"Master Potter?" I'm not following.

"God," he answers simply. "How He molds us into something from nothing. I guess I wanted to try to understand Him more after everything."

I haven't been to church in years, well, really since my dad died. Kevin and I went to church on Sundays with him while my mom stayed home. It's not that I've forgotten about God. I believe He exists, believe my dad is in a better place. I don't even blame God for the cancer. Even at seventeen, I knew how broken our world was. I just kind of leaned more away from, than into, God. Still appreciating Him, but not exactly seeking Him out.

"So, did it help?" I ask.

"I'm still in the process of understanding. Not sure I'll ever *not* be in that process," he says softly.

"So, what did you do before pottery?"

"I was a surgeon, actually," he answers, and my mind flip-flops.

"An actual surgeon? Like scrubs, mask, that funny looking cap, scissors, and real-live surgery where you cut people open and fix them?" I ramble, because honestly, I don't know what else to do. Boone does not look like a surgeon at all. Not that I know what all surgeons look like. I've never had surgery.

"No, I meant the game of Operation," he teases, standing up to poke at the logs in the fireplace.

"It's just, you don't seem the surgeon type," I say.

He nods his head. "Well, I was once Dr. Montgomery."

"So, do you miss it?" I ask, watching as the sparks sprinkle like flaming confetti as the logs move around.

Boone gently places a new log on the fire. "Not really. I worked hard for it—thirteen years of school and residency, but I don't really wish I was back in an operating room."

"That's a long time," I say. My schooling took four years, and yes, I worked hard to climb the ladder to be where I am today, but the commitment didn't seem as intense as becoming a doctor.

"Well, enough about that. Can I ask you a question?" He brushes his hands against each other, flecks of bark falling to the ground.

"Sure."

"What's your favorite food?"

"Coffee," I answer swiftly.

"Coffee isn't a food."

"It literally comes from beans, Boone. It's 100 percent a food, and the majority of my daily caloric intake," I defensively argue.

"What's your favorite food?"

"Bananas."

I squint at him. "There are no bananas in this house."

"Well, I don't really like the bananas themselves. I like when I have bananas and I let them sit on my counter until they turn black, and my mom comes up and makes banana bread."

I internally grin at the thought of Boone buying bananas just so his mom can make him something he loves. "So, you're close with your family?"

He nods his head. "I am. I grew up around here and moved back after Becca. My parents have been happily married for forty-two years, and I have a younger sister, Camryn. She's married, has three kids and a goldfish. She lives out in California. I see my parents at least once a week and talk to Camryn often."

"Are they back for Christmas?"

Boone shakes his head. "Christmas in California with Trevor's family, my brother-in-law. It was just going to be me and my parents, not that I do Christmas. I just usually go eat."

I look around the room, thinking how perfect a tree would be in this space. It's practically made for Christmas. The fireplace is ideal for stockings, the mantle perfect for garland. I can see it all in my head, a cozy little Christmas. He really should do Christmas. I understand why he doesn't, but it's such a waste of a good cabin.

Boone's intently watching me. "So, what else about your family, besides your dad that I know you loved and your mom that you don't seem to as much?"

"I didn't really grow up in a family that felt complete, even though statistically we were a traditional family unit. My mother and dad stayed together, but they never seemed as if they wanted to be together. I have a younger brother, Kevin. Kevin and I are more than siblings; we're more like best friends. We do this thing at Christmas that we call Santa Secrets. We lie under the Christmas tree and reveal all the things we've kept from each other all year. We started doing it when I was nine and he was seven. My dad had told us that Santa gave the best presents to truth tellers, so we figured it was our last-ditch effort to get all the truth out before Santa came." I smile at the memory that has become tradition.

"You still do that?" Boone questions.

I nod my head. "Oh yes. The secrets have gotten better each year. Sometimes we intentionally keep something from each other just so we have something big to reveal at Christmas."

"Honest Kate keeping secrets?" Boone teases me, the left side of his mouth turned up into a lopsided grin.

"Hardest thing I do all year," I laugh. "Okay, ask me something else. Something beyond the skin-deep things of family and food. Not that I don't think your favorite color or place to vacation would be interesting, but..."

"Green, I don't vacation, and what's with the bird tattoo?"

The question makes me swallow hard and pull my mouth into a tight line. I knew he'd most likely seen it. It's a little hard to miss, especially when a man had to undress and redress you like a floppy, lifeless Barbie doll.

"My dad loved bluebirds," I mutter.

"But the placement..." His words trail off.

"I'm aware." I cross my arms and lean back into the sofa.

"It's just a little weird if it's a memorial tattoo and it's on your lower back..." The corner of his lip is twitching upward, and there's a sparkle in his eyes, that while I'm completely humiliated, creates an urge to make him smile.

"It was the 2000s," I explain. "I mean, really, we were completely unhinged during that time. Plucking each other's eyebrows like we were a Mrs. Potato Head; wearing bright blue eyeshadow that, let's be honest, no one in this world can pull off; and dropping it low when everyone needed to stay up."

Success. The twitch grows into a grin. "But the clouds kind of make it look like..."

At this, my face warms. "I'm aware. It's an unfortunate placement, but I was only seventeen."

"You have to be eighteen to get a tattoo unless your mom..."

The thought of my mother signing off on a tattoo makes me give a stiff laugh. "Ha! No. My mother still has no idea it exists. And yes, I was seventeen, which should indicate the type of tattoo artist I went to, which then would explain the fact that the clouds do not look like clouds and more just like wind."

Boone laughs, but it's not like a laugh I've heard yet. It's deep and rich and more stimulating than the first sip of coffee in the morning. It echoes in the small room, and I don't mind being surrounded by it. In fact, I want that sound to bundle around me so I can relax into it.

"You know, you can have it removed. Have a new tattoo done in his honor."

"I don't know. While this one is embarrassing, it tells a story of a seventeen-year-old girl that was grieving deeply and needed something permanent that made her feel in control when she felt anything but. Although I can't exactly see it, I know it's there. Erasing it seems like erasing who I once was. Who I needed to be then to become who I am now."

Boone tilts his head. His blue eyes narrow in that way where you feel someone is really looking at you, trying to peer deeper into your delirious ramblings. "You are an interesting woman, Kate."

"Interesting in a good way?" I question, tucking a loose strand of hair behind my ear.

"I haven't yet decided," he admits.

"You're interesting, too," I shoot back.

"Interesting in a good way?" he asks.

"I haven't yet decided," I repeat with a small shoulder shrug and a smile.

Chapter Twelve

I'm trying not to think about how Boone's sheets are wrapped around me, how I lost a fight about who got the bed while my fingers were covered in sticky dough while forming cinnamon rolls, or how in the span of hours, a stranger figured out how to remove my armor of fast-talking honesty to find flesh and feelings beneath it all.

It's why I can't go to sleep even though I've had my eyes closed for what I calculate is at least forty-five minutes. It's why when I hear Boone enter the bedroom, I keep my eyes tightly shut. Even when I can feel him near me. Even when he quietly kneels beside me. Even when he gently rubs the area around the gash on my head as if his thumb is a feather.

But then his hand is heavy on my arm, my arm that I am using all my brain power to send a signal of instruction to relax, to tell it that it's supposed to be slumbering, that it can under no circumstances flinch or flex.

Boone sighs, and I feel like I'm in a moment that I shouldn't be in. That this is more about him than it should be about me. Or maybe I want it to be more about him than it is about me, but either way, I wish I was truly sleeping and not just faking it.

His gaze is practically piercing through my skin. I imagine him studying my every pore, every wrinkle, every scar from the ignorant teenage phase I went through where I stabbed my pimples open with a safety pin.

Minutes go by that feel like hours, until his sigh grows wearier, and I hear the subtle sound of his lips parting. "Lord, I'm going to start with the easy. Place your healing hand on Kate, physically and emotionally. I can tell she worries more than she lets on, that she's searching for answers just like I am. Wondering what is real and what is not. I don't know her, and yet I feel like I do. But Lord, You sure gave her a few more words than most when You made her."

Without seeing Boone, I can hear the way his lips curve out in a soft smile, and I try my hardest to still every goosebump that has raised even the smallest hairs on my skin, to calm my heartbeat that has begun to pound hard against my chest. This man is praying for me, and I'm not sure I've been prayed over since I lost my dad.

"Now for the hard," he whispers into the space around us that has somehow grown heavy and light at the same time, this moment imprinting itself on my very soul. "Lord, You know I don't believe that everything happens for a reason. There isn't a reason You can give me that is good enough for losing Becca, but maybe some things do happen for a reason. Maybe Kate happened for a reason. Maybe, if only to remind me that I have a lot of life left to live. For her to remind me that the time she had with her dad was a gift, and she was grateful to be loved by him for that long."

Then his hushed voice cracks, and Boone is soon crying. I can feel it in the way his hand softly shakes against my arm. It's subtle, but it's there. And I fight every urge I have to pop open my eyes and pull this emotionally exposed man into an embrace. But I also know how much that could complicate things. How that intimate experience could rip the quilt I've constructed of my life in neat little squares into shreds.

"And maybe, Lord, maybe Kate happened for more. Lord, you know I'm fine staying stuck right here until my last breath leaves my bones, but if I'm not meant to be here, help me find the footsteps forward. And let Kate find confidence in her footsteps forward, too. She's special, and she deserves to know that and walk that out."

The floorboards beneath Boone's knees groan as his body shifts. His thumb rubs gently in circles, making the soft fabric of the thermal pajamas he lent me scratch against my goosebumps.

And then Boone sighs, "Amen," and the heated friction of his hand is gone, along with the rest of him.

But what doesn't leave me is that Boone just told God I was special.

Out loud.

And I don't know what to do with that. I haven't felt special in a long time. Not to anyone. Not even to myself. And if Boone thinks I'm special, then he's not trying to figure out if I'm interesting. He already thinks I am, and that's a problem because if I'm honest with myself, I'm not trying to figure out if Boone is interesting either. He is.

CHAPTER THIRTEEN

M y nose wakes up before the rest of my body does, sending a rush of desire pulsing through my veins that rouses the rest of my senses. I hear the crackling of a fire and then something I haven't heard yet. A gentle, deep humming, and... surely, it's not from Boone?

My eyelids flutter open just barely before I sit up and swing my legs over the side of the bed. I pick up my phone and feel my eyes enlarging from the numbers. It's ten o'clock. I can't remember the last time I slept past six. There isn't exactly an excess quantity of time when you live in New York City. There are lines to wait in, cabs to catch, and it takes me a good three hours every morning just to get to work.

I slide across the wood floor in Boone's wool socks, toward the living room, following the smell of coffee and the sound of what sounds like melodious murmuring of a Christmas carol, so it definitely cannot be Boone.

But when I peek around the doorway, I can literally feel my jaw drop.

There's Boone, steaming coffee mug in hand, Dog curled up

next to him on the couch, and a Christmas tree that smells fresh from the woods. It's strung with lights that look familiar, but I can't place them.

"What is happening?" I question, my arms hanging floppy at my sides as if I'm lifeless, and maybe I am. Maybe this is a dream? It must be a dream.

"Good morning, Kate." Boone smiles. "Coffee?"

I nod my head. "Yes, of course. Duh. But what is all this?"

"Did you just *duh* me?" Boone asks as he stands from the couch. Dog stretches out, his black fur glistening from the glow of the Christmas lights, yawning.

"I did. I most definitely *duh*'d you, because it was an unnecessary question. But what isn't an unnecessary question is why is there a Christmas tree in your living room?" I walk over to it slowly, as if it's a mythical creature and not just a simple pine tree.

"Well, I figured it's not just me for Christmas this year." He shrugs his shoulders. "Gingerbread creamer?"

I nod my head again. "These lights?"

I reach out to touch them. I've seen them somewhere, but where would Boone have gotten them? We're snowed in.

"The hens weren't too happy I stole them from their coop, but I figured they could do without them for a day or two," Boone answers. "I'll be right back with coffee."

Boone cut down a tree and strung it with his chicken-coop lights. For me.

Not for him. Not for Dog. Not for Christmas.

For me.

This man makes it too easy to like him.

I walk over to the couch, grabbing a plaid blanket to wrap around me, and snuggle down next to the cat. "What do you think, Dog? Christmas is better with a tree, right?"

He pushes his head against my leg, purring. I take the movement and sound as a yes.

Boone reenters the room, a cup of angelic liquid gripped in his hands. "Merry Christmas Eve, Kate."

I take the coffee, inhaling it for a good ten seconds before I reply, "Merry Christmas Eve, Boone. Thanks for the coffee and the tree. Although I'm a little nervous about how Goose will treat me now since she already hates me. If she knows I'm the reason you stole her lights, then I can only imagine it will sharpen her animosity toward me, and by sharpen, I mean her claws won't miss next time she attacks me."

Boone picks up Dog, moving him over to the other side so he can sit right beside me. Then, he reaches over, brushing hair that has fallen over my eyes out of my face, and I'm positive that every atom in my body just burst from what feels like natural, gentle affection. Something I haven't had in a long time. I feel everything.

"Goose doesn't hate you. She can share her light for a little while," Boone says softly.

And the words feel like they mean something more than just a conversation about a chicken. They feel like Boone didn't just take an axe to a tree last night, but that he took one to his heart, too—splitting it open to hope and possibility.

But I'll soon be gone, and I can't be the one that breaks Boone's heart after all he's been through. It's not fair to him. It's not fair to me. Do I even want this, or is it just being snowed in at Christmas with this handsome lumberjack of a man that has the inside of me currently lit up like a Christmas tree?

"Boone, don't take this the wrong way," I begin. "I like you. I really do, but..."

His facial features rearrange themselves into one of quick confusion.

"You can't kiss me, and if I happen to slip and fall into this Christmas magic you are creating—which it's working, by the way—don't kiss me back. *Please*, don't kiss me back. I won't be able to catch my breath if you do, and I need to. I have a life back in New York. A life I like that would just complicate this life that you like here in the mountains."

"You're asking me not to kiss you?" Boone questions, tilting his head.

"And to not kiss me back if I kiss you," I add on.

"Do you want to kiss me?" he asks.

I bite my bottom lip, strategically sorting through my words before I spit them all out, while watching Boone intently.

He doesn't look offended. In fact, he looks even more intrigued, which is not exactly the look I was hoping for. Like he wants to kiss me just to find out what I'd actually do. Would I kiss him back?

Yes. Yes, I would. But I need to ask him to have more strength than I currently possess. I mean, I did almost die recently. I'm kind of the weaker one of the two of us. I think.

"Boone, you're a super likeable person. Perhaps the most likeable person I've ever met. Of course I want to kiss you. You've got that mysterious mountain-man appeal. You make the most delicious coffee I've ever tasted. You seem content to be with yourself. You cut me down a tree. You saved my life. I mean, it's kind of the perfect combination of everything to inspire the wistful desire to put my lips on your lips. To see what it'd be like. But we both know this isn't a good idea. Yeah, sure, it could be great. But Boone, I'm not looking for great. I don't date. I'm not searching for a man to take care of me. I can and want to take care of myself."

"But you want to kiss me?" Boone questions again.

"Is that all you got from that?"

Boone smirks, and unfortunately it makes me want to kiss him more. "I promise I won't kiss you back, but I'm not that likeable of a person, Kate. I hate jury duty, so twice I've just sided with the accused to get out of it. I also forget my mom's birthday every year. June third. Oh, yes. I know it now, but I forget it every June. My dad calls me and reminds me on the day of, because quite honestly, he forgets, too. I also don't recycle. I know. It's terrible. I throw plastic in the trash can."

"You're not helping your case, Boone," I laugh. "You just made me like you more."

"We're adults, Kate. I don't think a kiss is going to ruin things for us," Boone suggests.

I take a sip of coffee that wraps my tongue up in warmth and joy and relax into it. Then I look at Boone seriously. "I like my life, Boone, and kissing you seems like it might ruin things for me, or at least complicate things. So, let's just enjoy Christmas together without any kissing, and as soon as I can catch a flight, I'll go back to the city, and you can forget about the ridiculous woman you had to rescue because she needed coffee." Then I tip my mug toward him. "This is great, as usual. Thank you. I'm going to go check on the cinnamon rolls."

Then I stand up and leave the room, because if I don't, I'm not sure I'm strong enough to find any other reasons to argue against kissing Boone. Not right now. Not without at least three more cups of coffee in me.

Chapter Fourteen

Three cups of coffee later, and my feelings are less wobbly.

That, and I booked a flight for December twenty-sixth at six in the morning. Putting an end date on this cozy, unplanned escape from reality in the mountains helps me focus on what is to come. I'm going to fly back to New York, and then in a week will fly into Tulsa to spend some time with my brother and his family.

That's where I need to be.

My phone rings with Kevin's name on the screen.

"Hey, Kev," I answer.

"You sure you can't make it to Mom's?" he asks, an incredulous tone to his question. As if he doesn't believe I'm really stuck in the mountains. As if he thinks I've made this whole thing up to avoid our mother. Which, I would do if I didn't love my brother as much as I do.

"Hold on," I say before I put my hand over the phone. "Boone! Come here!"

Boone is there in less than ten seconds, running into the living room from the kitchen. "What? Is something wrong?"

"Only that my brother doesn't believe I can't make it to my mother's for Christmas. Mind taking a selfie with me to prove that I am indeed here in the mountains with a stranger?" I ask.

He shrugs his shoulders. "Sure."

I hold the phone out at the perfect height, angling down slightly at us. Boone steps behind me, and I lean back into him, his beard scratching up against my cheek. I can feel the heat beginning to swirl between us as I argue with my body about not relaxing into his. "Smile!"

We both grin at the camera. It flashes and I quickly step away from Boone, sending the photo to my brother before putting the phone back up to my ear. "See. I'm here with Boone. In the mountains. Snowed in. I can't make it home for Christmas."

Then Boone takes the phone from me, and I give him an appalling look that makes his dimples appear. "Hey, Kevin. It's Boone Montgomery. Yeah. Unfortunately, the roads haven't been cleared yet; although, they are working to get to it today from what I've heard."

Then Boone laughs, and I hate that I can't hear what my brother is saying. Boone looks over at me, twinkling as brightly as the Rockefeller Center Christmas Tree. It's my favorite Christmas tree. Well, *was* my favorite. At the moment, I'm a big fan of the tree in Boone's cabin that's strung with chicken coop lights. "She told me I couldn't. I'm afraid so. Yeah. You'll have to ask her about it. It was her versus a chicken. Good to talk to you, too."

Boone extends the phone to me with a laugh and then leaves the room.

"What did you say to him?!" I demand from my brother.

"First of all, did you lose a chicken fight? That gash on your head looks pretty intense."

"Yes. The chicken's name is Goose, and she wasn't a fan of me being in her coop. I fell and caught my head on a board," I explain quickly. "Now, what did you say to Boone?"

"I have more questions about a chicken named Goose for later. Mark that down in your brain for New Year's. And I just told him to kiss you, but he informed me you've already told him he can't. Such a shame, too. A little romance in the mountains would be good for you," Kevin rambles.

"You're literally telling a *stranger* to kiss me," I remind him.

"The photo didn't exactly exude stranger danger, Kate. In fact, it looks like it could be kind of the opposite," he teases. "Anyway, Merry Christmas. Don't waste this little situation of yours. What would Dad say?"

"He'd be more concerned than you are," I utter.

"He'd be concerned if you were concerned, but he'd also tell you that life is too short to waste it not living it with the ones you love most. He learned the hard way, Kate. We both know that. Mom even knows that." Kevin's voice has morphed into one of honesty.

Our mother did know. Dad stayed with her, but he didn't love her. In his defense, she didn't love him back. Dad stayed for us. He thought he was doing the best thing, especially when he was diagnosed with cancer. He didn't want to die alone, and he wanted to make sure our mother was taken care of. He did love her in that way, in the way his marriage vows had bonded his life to hers.

"That's why I'll be at your place for New Year's. I won't miss out on the ones I love most," I reply.

"Kate, I say this because I love you. No matter how amazing Maisy Jo, the kids, and I are, you deserve more than that. You deserve what I have even if you don't feel like you do. Letting someone else love you doesn't mean you have to lose yourself to them. Loving the right person makes you believe in yourself more, even love yourself more."

"See you soon, Kev. Merry Christmas," I say before I end the call so I can end his reasoning. I don't want to hear it.

He knows exactly what one of my biggest fears is, the fear I've been avoiding wrestling with since Boone prayed over me last night. Since I felt something more than just liking Boone, but the idea of being with Boone. Those silly Santa Secret nights as kids and adults have bonded us to the innermost workings of our heads and hearts, and now, my brother has voiced my fear out loud, so I can't avoid it.

"Your brother seems nice." Boone steps back into the living room with another cup of coffee. It seems we both are consuming quite a bit of the energizing liquid, and I try not to think if it's because we'd rather be awake to spend time together instead of asleep.

"Whatever he told you..." I trail off.

"I made a promise, Kate," Boone replies, stepping closer to me. Too close. "Although, maybe breaking promises is one of the things that makes me a less likeable person. If I add that to the list, will that make you like me as much?"

His coffee cup is steaming my face like the best facial I've ever received. Definitely the best smelling one. I take the cup from him, my hands slipping beneath his. I bite my tongue at the tingling my nerves experience before taking a sip of his coffee, watching as his mouth pulls tight into a grin. He chose peppermint creamer, and it's delicious.

"That wasn't yours, you know," he remarks as he runs his hand through his beard.

I shrug my shoulders as I take another sip before I say, "I did know, but you didn't exactly stop me."

He steps closer, which I didn't think was possible. Our bodies are millimeters from brushing up against each other, the coffee mug strangled between us.

"So, do you like the Christmas tree?" His voice is a throaty whisper, making my knees plead with me to quiver, but I won't let them.

And I shouldn't have taken his coffee. It was a bold, stupid move, but I wanted to see how he'd react, and unfortunately, he took the challenge and made me regret it with his lips hovering too close to mine.

I take a step back from Boone. "Of course, I like the Christmas tree. No sane person would say they didn't like the tree that you went out and chopped down in the middle of the night with your axe like some muscular version of the Grinch when his heart grew three sizes attempting to restore Christmas."

"But are you a sane person?" Boone teases, which causes playful irritation to twitch up my spine, eliciting a response of softly punching his bicep.

"I may be crazy in some ways, but I'm sane in the right ones," I clarify.

"Fair enough," Boone replies before snatching the coffee out of my hands and taking his own sip.

We're now not just sharing Christmas, air, and clothes;we're sharing coffee, and that seems like one of the most intimate things I've done with a man in years, causing me to realize that Boone isn't the only one melting. With all the melting between us, it's only a matter of time until the winter wonderland we are stuck in becomes summer.

"I think I need some air," I say. "We've been stuck inside for too long. Got any ideas?"

His lips pull up in a smile. "I've got a couple."

CHAPTER FIFTEEN

The sun glitters on the untouched snow. I'm not sure I've seen untouched snow in New York City. It's always pushed and shoved to the sides to make way for the hustle and bustle. No time to just let it be, to enjoy it, to realize how intricately designed it really is. I used to love snow. Now, too often, I just see it as an inconvenience.

We've hiked a bit to a clearing, where the trees surround us, but we can still see the smoke curling from the chimney back at the cabin.

Boone scoops up a handful of snow. "Look."

I lean over slightly.

"Closer," he requests.

So, I get closer, my face hovering inches above his hand, trying to dissect the small pile of flakes. "See how different each snowflake is? Not imperfect because of their differences but made more perfect because of them. I think about that a lot when I'm throwing clay on the wheel. I don't have to create the same thing twice. There's a beauty in that. How God just makes things differently, yet they belong together."

I sigh to myself. I should've known Boone was going to find ways to continue talking about us. This man doesn't seem like one that gives up easily. We at least have that in common.

"We don't belong together, Boone. We're just different," I reply.

"I didn't say anything about us." He grins. "Still thinking about us, huh?"

I shake my head. "No."

Then suddenly, the snow is in my face. From Boone's glove.

"You didn't!?" I scream, taking my own glove to wipe the snow from my exposed skin.

"What about now?" He laughs. "Do you still want to kiss me, Kate?"

More than anything that's what I want to do, but my coffee intake sobered me up from making any decisions based on feelings instead of facts.

"Unfair advantages for a snowball fight, Boone. I can't exactly run away in your boots that are made for the feet of giants," I argue. "Plus, how old are we? This seems a bit childish."

His chin lowers, along with his tone. "Well, I'm forty-one, and I've yet to think a snowball fight is solely reserved for children. Are you going to let something as trivial as a number keep you from having fun?"

I haven't asked his age yet, so I am a bit surprised. He doesn't look like he is forty-one. He doesn't seem older than I am, and yet, what really is age? Boone's right...it's a number, a number that we define our existence by. A number that tells us how many years we've lived but also a number in which we assume how many years we have left. A number that sometimes keeps us from believing there's nothing left for us because the world continually informs us that our number isn't small enough. It's one place where the world believes less is more.

My dad was forty-two when he died, which is a strange thing to realize. That this man in front of me, cheeks glowing and red from the Christmas Eve snow, is almost the last age my dad had ever known on this earth. And what would my dad have done right now? What would he expect from his Katydilla?

I bend over and scoop up snow, quickly packing it into a ball in my hands. I look over at Boone where the glow has now migrated to his blue eyes. He's grinning at me, forcing me to swallow down my own smile.

"I'll go easy on you, Kate," he says before he bends over making his own snowball.

"I don't think so, sir," I spout. "I'm perfectly capable of holding my own without you handicapping yourself."

"But, as you said, this isn't fair. You're handicapped by wearing my boots," he remarks while he makes another snowball, placing it in his pile while I do the same.

"Fine. I get three extra snowballs, and I get to throw first," I instruct.

"Deal. I'll make fifteen, and you make eighteen?"

"Perfect," I reply as I forcefully pack together another snowball, praying my aim is as good as it once was when I used to absolutely obliterate my brother. He never could win a competition against me. Snowball fights. Board games. Who could swim the most laps around the pool. I was even better at sneaking back in when we'd been to the same party. He'd always get caught, but he never ratted me out.

Minutes later, I have my stack of eighteen. I look down at Boone's massive black galoshes on my feet. "Boots, please don't fail me again."

At least if these boots do betray me once more, I will only plummet toward soft snow, but unfortunately, they will also take my pride down with me.

"Ready?" Boone calls out from about twenty feet away.

"I was born ready," I declare through gritted teeth.

So far, this man has saved me from a freezing death in a blizzard, has tended to a gash on my forehead from stumbling in his chicken coop, and has rescued me from his shower of death. But while I have survived all the incidents, I have not saved myself from embarrassment. I cannot create another reason for which Boone has to rescue me.

"You get the first throw," Boone yells with his hands stretched out, making him an easy target. "Take your best shot."

I pick up a snowball, tossing it from gloved hand to gloved hand, getting a feel for its weight and hoping twelve-year-old me emerges in energy and ability.

"You've got this Kate," I whisper to myself.

"Did you say something?" Boone bellows.

But instead of repeating myself, I pull my arm back, squinting at Boone for aim, and hurl a snowball through the air. It sails high above Boone as he ducks and rolls toward his pile, picking one up as he jumps back up and catches me in the gut. Fortunately, I'm wearing Boone's clothes, which means there is a lot of material, and I barely feel the blow.

I quickly fill my arms full of snowballs, chucking them as fast as I can. Catching him in the arm, the leg, the chest, and my favorite—smack dab in the middle of his face.

He laughs that deep laugh of his, and the wide space around us consumes it into the blue skies above, making me feel like the angels can hear his childlike joy at something so simple.

When was the last time I laughed at something simple?

But I don't have time to think about it, because soon Boone is on the attack, and I realize I've already used the majority of my snowballs, so I start running as fast as one can when they are wearing oversized boots that devour one's entire legs. I'm just Kate—head, torso, and black boots.

"Ah!" I scream out as Boone catches me in the back with a forceful snowball.

"Better figure out a plan, Kate. I'm afraid I've got more ammo than you," Boone boasts.

"But I've already hit you four times," I shout while still running away from him.

"I've gotten you three," he teases loudly. He isn't even breathing hard like I am, no huffing to his breath. Benefit of the mountain-man physique. "And I've got three times as many snowballs left."

My brain starts sorting through my ideas file on how to proceed from here so I don't lose, because if there's anything I'm terrible at...it's losing. It's not necessarily the best quality of mine, but I've always been a sore loser. I can pout for days, mope around in pajamas like it's a career, and consume enough pints of ice cream that my brother informs me I need my own milk cow.

Finally, something clicks. We never said anything about stealing one another's ammo. And what were the snowball fight rules, really? With a plan revolving in my brain, I energetically curve back around toward where Boone's pile is left unattended.

"Hey!" Boone shouts, as if he knows exactly what I'm about to do.

As I'm running, I kick off the boots that are causing more problems than not and pick up speed now that I'm only in wool socks. It'll be worth the cold feet to defeat Boone.

I arrive at his pile and begin picking up the snowballs as fast as possible, releasing them toward Boone, who is quickly closing the gap between us. I hit him not once, not twice, but four more times. I give a mighty war cry as I throw the last one. He's only seven or eight feet from me, and it plummets into his face, covering his beard in beaded icicles.

But then Boone does something I don't expect.

He tackles me to the ground. It's gentle yet forceful as the snow curls around my body. And Boone is lying on top of me, smiling from ear to ear. "Cheater."

"Not technically. And that's nine to your three." I smirk. "Loser."

"You're impossible." He sighs as he stares at me, his blue eyes becoming one with the sky above him.

Then he lifts himself up just enough to use his hand to brush hair and snow from my face softly. His hand lingers as it traces down the side of my face to my chin, and my brain bypasses all facts to feelings as it plays an imaginative movie reel where Boone's thumb gently brushes against my lips before he bends down and kisses me. And it's warm, perfect, and makes me forget that my toes are freezing in Boone's soaking wool socks.

But he doesn't kiss me, even though I watch as his eyes flicker down to my lips, and I wonder if he's imagining the same thing I am.

Instead, he jumps up, offering his hand to pull me up. "We better get you inside before you lose your feet to frostbite. You've already attempted that once."

Boone isn't going to break his promise, and I kind of wish he would, but I also know he shouldn't. He can't. I have a life back in New York City, and as many times as I've tried to puzzle Boone and I together in the last several hours, I can't quite get all our edges to fit. Someone will get hurt, and I don't want it to be either of us.

CHAPTER SIXTEEN

"I booked a flight for the twenty-sixth at six a.m.," I state as I pull on a dry pair of Boone's wool socks. I'm beginning to get used to this very low-key, comfy status I've developed in his cabin. Although, I really wish he would have thought to rescue my bag when he rescued me, if only for the mascara and facial scrub.

"Still going to fly to your mom's?" he asks.

"Oh no," I snap quickly. "Straight back to New York, and then I'll go see my brother and his family for New Year's."

Boone nods his head as he stokes the fire. "I heard the roads will be cleared by this evening."

"Oh," I mutter. "There weren't any flights on Christmas Day."

"I didn't mean you had to leave on Christmas," Boone says swiftly before putting the iron poker back in its holder. His arms are crossed now as he looks down at me sitting on the couch. I wish I could read his mind, read the script that is typing out inside his head right now. "I was just letting you know the roads will be cleared. I'll be able to get you to the airport."

I swallow. "Oh, good. Perfect, actually, since I wasn't sure how I was going to get there. I don't suppose you have Uber here."

"Afraid not," he replies as Dog rubs up against his legs.

My eyes slowly trace upward, from the cat to Boone. He's wearing another red-and-black flannel, and I'm positive that if I opened his closet there would be hangers full of the same outfit, but I like it. In fact, I can't imagine Boone in anything else, especially scrubs. It makes me wonder how much of him has changed from who he once was or if he just dresses differently.

"So, have you always had a beard?" I question.

"What?" He uncrosses his arms and strides toward me. I quickly pull my legs up to my chest, twisting to face him as he sits down on the couch beside me. I at least need my legs to be a barrier after all the foolish friction between us today.

"It's just, I can't envision you in scrubs. You don't seem like the doctor type that would be bending over with a scalpel and murmuring instructions to others around you as you work quickly to save someone's life under fluorescent light," I ramble. "I mean, I can't see the mask and goggles and the beard exactly going together."

Boone's laugh is more of a sigh. "No, I didn't have a beard."

I squint my eyes, trying to pluck Boone's beard from his face in my mind. I can't do it. "I can't see you without a beard."

Boone reaches into his pocket, pulling out his phone. I glance over my knees, watching his thumb as it moves across the screen before he hands the phone over to me. "Here."

And there is Boone, well, a version of Boone that looks more like a brother or cousin than Boone. His face is clean shaven, but those are his blue eyes. He looks smaller, younger, and yet, when I look at

Boone now and Boone then, he still seems joyful, even after what he's been through.

"Where did you live?" I question as I continue examining the photograph where he's wearing slacks and a polo, his hands in his pockets, and he's smiling the kind of smile that you only give to someone you love. I wonder if Becca was behind the camera.

"California," he answers.

I nod my head. "Your sister is out in California."

"She is," he replies.

"Was Becca from California?" I watch Boone as I say her name, to read his expression for any indication about how he feels about me picking at the edges of memories, of his life before.

The lines around his eyes soften. "Yes. I met Becca in college. She was a California girl through and through, and I couldn't get her to leave even though I'll always prefer the mountains to the beach." Then Boone leans over and swipes at the screen. "There she is."

And she is there, on his phone screen, radiantly glowing, smiling at me. Tanned skin and legs up to her ears. Long dark hair but highlighted perfectly by the sun or by the expert touch of a fantastic hairdresser. Her face is thin, lips full, eyes matching blue to his. Cut-off shorts and a white tank top. "She's beautiful, Boone."

I can picture them together. Their towering heights, dark hair, and impeccable features. They would have had beautiful babies.

But I don't want to just picture them together, I want to see them, so I find my thumb taking orders from my brain before reason can interfere, and I swipe through the photos until I land on one of them. Boone's watching me, not stopping me. Completely at peace with me peeking within what was once his heart, and maybe still is. Or at least, still part of it.

And I was right. A picture of them together, not smiling at the camera but instead at each other, appears. Arms wrapped around waists, heads touching. They had been perfect.

It's a weird feeling—seeing what was and knowing that it had been completely devastated in one moment. Boone had a life and had most likely planned out this amazing future with this perfect woman that probably didn't talk as much as I did, or toe the line when you weren't supposed to, or laugh at times when it was really inappropriate to do so.

I've never loved anyone in that way. The way that you begin to create a scrapbook of memories that could be. I've always been what men had said was too much or too controlling or too ambitious or too loud or just too anything.

And I don't want to compare myself to Becca. It isn't fair to me, and it isn't fair to Boone, and it really isn't fair to Becca. She isn't here to defend herself, to reveal all her own insecurities, to humanize herself. Instead, she's an angel, and my brain shouldn't be figuring out how I compete with that. But it is. It's what I've always done, and it's what I've conditioned it to do.

Everything in life is a competition. It's Kate Everett against the world after all.

Then my eyes crawl up to the corner of the screen, and I shriek, jumping up from the couch. "How is it already after four?!"

"Is that a problem?" Boone asks with no alarm to his tone as I hand him back his phone.

"I better start working on our Christmas Eve dinner, or we won't have one."

Plus, I need the distraction, and cooking is always something that helps me focus on one feeling instead of all the others—hunger.

I start to march toward the kitchen, putting a plan together of what I need to begin with first. I am planning on making a couple ham steaks I found in the freezer that I moved to the fridge last night, mashed potatoes, canned corn, and cinnamon rolls. It isn't much, but I think it is a decent meal, considering I'm shopping in Boone's fridge and cabinet that pretended to be a pantry.

"Can I help?"

I look around nervously. I mean, what else is he really supposed to do? One can only poke at the fire so many times.

"Um," I utter. "Sure."

"You don't really sound *sure* about that," Boone remarks, still sitting on the couch. "Haven't I proven myself worthy after the omelet lesson?"

His comment cracks my lips into a small smile. "Yes."

"I'll make you another cup of coffee, too, if bribery works," he suggests as he stands.

"You know I can't say no to coffee," I say while tilting my head at him.

"I know," he replies. "You're not so hard to figure out, Kate."

"Oh, is that so?" I raise my voice, slightly offended that he thinks he has me all figured out.

"None of us really are, if that makes you feel better," he teases as he reaches me.

And I suppose he's right. We all like to think we are more complicated than we really are, creating mysteries within the fabric of our being, hoping people find us more interesting than the next person. But really, we're all more of the same than we want to admit. Fears, insecurities, and feelings fluttering beneath our chests. I can't fault him for the honesty, not when I pride myself on it.

"I'd feel better if there was a latte with gingerbread creamer in my hand right now," I mutter as I look down at my empty palms.

"On it." He laughs as he makes his way to the kitchen first.

I hear the espresso machine grinding beans, and I can't help but wonder if he made coffee for Becca every morning. What kind of husband he had been. What kind of life he would have had with her.

And if he had a life with me, what would that look like, and would he wonder if it was as good of a life as he had hoped for with Becca...

Again, unfair comparisons, but my brain is wired for it.

It doesn't matter anyway. Tomorrow is Christmas, and then I'm flying out the next morning. We have thirty-six hours left together. Thirty-six hours is nothing. It's practically already over.

And yet...life can change in less than that.

Can I be honest with myself for thirty-six more hours? Honest with my feelings? Feelings that feel more like I'm not really scared of being with Boone. I'm scared of what my brother said earlier—the fear he'd unleashed audibly.

Loving someone means taking a risk, and it's not that I love Boone now, but isn't that the hope that comes with liking someone? And when you risk love, you risk loss.

Boone had already lost once, and I wasn't sure I was willing to risk myself or him to that. If he'd even choose to love me when he really got to know me.

He may be right that we're all not that hard to figure out, but the beginning of something always seems more magical than the middle of it.

CHAPTER SEVENTEEN

My insides are bursting. Boone and I somehow whipped up what I would consider to be in my top five Christmas Eve dinners, and that's saying a lot as my mother always has them catered in from some of the best chefs in the area. Not that our area was ever prominent in fine dining, but they were still home cooked and fabulous.

I'm lying on the floor, my head under the tree as I look up at its branches draped with the chicken-coop lights. It smells amazing. I never had real Christmas trees growing up. My dad would hang those silly pine-scented car air fresheners on the branches, claiming that it was just as good as the real thing. It's not, I now realize.

Dog has curled up next to me, a welcome warmth as he purrs happily. Boone had even prepared the cat a small Christmas Eve meal with ham and mashed potatoes. He'd devoured it.

I hear Boone's steady footsteps enter the living room from his bedroom. He'd taken a shower after dinner. I still have trust issues with the pipes and haven't braved challenging them again.

"What are you doing?" Boone asks, as he crouches down to look at me under the tree.

"Appreciating the tree," I answer.

"And you have to do it from under it?" he questions, his face rippling into wrinkles.

I smile more at myself than Boone. I reach my hand out at him, inviting him under the tree with me. "Come and gain a new perspective."

Boone doesn't answer with words. Instead, he grabs my hand and slides effortlessly under the tree with me. I can smell his soap that I never got to fully appreciate in my own shower when it attacked me yesterday. He keeps hold of my hand as he breathes out what seems like every ounce of air from his chest, relaxing onto the floor.

I roll my head over to look at him. "This is what Kevin and I do every Christmas Eve when we do Santa Secrets. It feels like we're somewhere else, somewhere closer to the magic of Christmas. We used to think Santa had a better chance of hearing us if we could speak into the tree. It's silly, I know. But there is something about lying here that makes the rest of everything feel far away. That somehow our secrets were safe under the tree together."

He rolls his head over, his blue eyes gentle as they gaze into my green ones. "That's not silly at all. It's special."

I smile at him. "What's silly is two adults still believing it."

He squeezes my hand. "So, let's do it."

"Let's do what?"

"Santa Secrets," he answers. "How's it work?"

"We don't have to tell each other all our secrets," I say quickly. "I'm not sure you can handle all my deepest secrets, anyway. I'm a lot."

"A lot of what?" he asks.

"You know what I mean," I mumble. "A lot of everything."

"Why do you say that as if it's something that's wrong with you? I've yet to be disappointed when there is a lot of something I like."

"You can't like me, Boone," I state as if it's a fact. As if I'm just naturally unlikeable, which statistically speaking, proves it. A lot of people have liked me and then fallen out of like fairly quickly.

"You can't tell me what I can and can't like, Kate," Boone argues.

"Well, then, let's do this, and we'll see if you still like me," I propose.

"What are the rules?" he asks promptly.

"It's secret for secret. That's it. Those are the rules," I explain.

"Are we allowed questions?"

"Questions?"

"Yeah, for clarification, or maybe to dig deeper into the secret."

"Yes," I answer. "That's fine. Let no secret detail go unturned."

He squeezes my hand again, which is something I've been trying to not think about. That we're holding hands. It seems like such a simple thing, and yet it doesn't seem simple with Boone. It seems real, and real is usually the opposite of simple. It's usually complicated and messy and, well, honest.

Which is why I haven't yet let go. I appreciate Boone's honesty, and if he wanted to let go, he would. I'm not going to be the first to break our honesty when the truth is, I want to hold his hand, too.

"You go first," he says. "You're the veteran."

I smirk. "Only by experience, not by age."

Boone laughs. "I wondered if you were going to say anything about my age reveal earlier. What do you think about it? Do I seem forty-one to you?"

"My dad was forty-two when he died," I reveal, which immediately sparks the reaction from Boone of squeezing my hand again. "But that's not my secret. Oh, I've got one. I called the police on my upstairs neighbors twice this year for loud music late at night. I thought they were having a party. Turns out, it was just their thirteen-year-old son learning to play the drums. Still, noisy, but I'm not one to discourage learning, so naturally, I had cookies made in the shape of drums and drumsticks for them and delivered the cookies myself."

"To apologize?" Boone asks.

"Oh, no. I didn't let them know it was me that called the police. To encourage their son—Liam, I learned—to keep up the good work. That I was a huge supporter of the musical arts," I add.

"Honest Kate wasn't honest?" Boone's eyes widen in amusement.

"Not when it meant having a tiff with my upstairs neighbors," I laugh. "Listen, enough people in New York are rude just for the fun of it. I didn't need people I lived in my building with to be rude for a reason."

"Fair enough," Boone agrees. "Plus, they got cookies."

"Exactly!" I exclaim. "Expensive ones, too. And now Liam even says hi to me in the elevator. Okay, your turn."

"Hmm," he mutters. "I don't do my own laundry, and I know, I'm a grown man who should be doing his own laundry, but I don't have a washer and dryer up here, and my mom insists. It's not that I can't do laundry. I can and have. It's just that I don't do it currently, or really for the last five years."

My eyebrows arch. "Your mom still does your laundry?"

"I know. It sounds bad, but it's not *still does*. She stopped when I moved to California. I had some unfortunate experiences with learning that you don't dump three capfuls of detergent in the washing machine and that it really does matter if you wash clothes on hot or cold. But when I moved back, my mom thought it was a way she could help me out while I was sorting out everything during that time, and she just never stopped."

"She seems like a good mom," I remark.

"She is," Boone agrees. "Keeps me in banana bread and clean clothes."

I smile at him. "My mother did my laundry when I lived at home, but only because she didn't want me to mess any of it up. She had strict rules for what was allowed to be worn to ensure my brother and I looked appropriate by her definition of it. When I was sixteen, I really wanted a pair of ripped jeans. Of course, she refused. Said they were pants for hoodlums. Soon after, my dad made up an excuse to get me out of school. He took me to the mall and bought me a pair. I kept them hidden in my Mustang and would change into them on my way to parties."

Boone laughs. "I think I would have liked your dad."

"He was a good person," I reply. "He wasn't perfect, but he was good."

"Those are the best kind of people," Boone remarks. "Now, your turn."

And because I like the shock-and-awe effect, I decide to reveal something that might scare Boone away. "I've never had a real boyfriend. I mean, I've had boyfriends and they were real, not imaginary. But not the kind of boyfriend where I thought it could be more—that it could be life. And I know that sounds ridiculous, because I'm fast approaching forty and you'd think...there would've at least been one."

"Did you love any of them?" Boone asks.

My eyebrows furrow together. "I mean, I liked them. I've even said, 'I love you' a few times and heard it back. But real love? No. Not the kind of love that actually means something bigger than a moment."

"It doesn't mean it's not for you, you know," he replies.

I feel the lines between my eyebrows crease more intensely.

"Love, Kate," Boone adds. "Just because you haven't had it yet, doesn't mean you won't. Love doesn't have an expiration date. Not in having it and not in losing it."

"Do you still love Becca?" I ask bluntly. I know he does, just like I still love my dad. But I need to hear him say it, instead of me just knowing it.

"I'll always love Becca. That doesn't mean it's the only love I'll have. I thought it was when I first came to this cabin five years ago. I kept hidden where love couldn't find me, but I've been wondering what's next for me. Praying about it," Boone says softly.

The truth is I'm not scared to kiss Boone. I'm not scared to love him, either. I'm scared that he'll eventually realize I'm not easy to love. It is easier to just not have it than to believe it can be for me.

"No one has wanted to try to love me like you love Becca. Something always happens where they realize I'm a lot to handle," I admit. "I mean, look at the predicament I got myself into by thinking I was bigger than a blizzard."

Boone smiles at me, but it's different. Tender. Something in the way his lips curve has softened. "Kate, it's not that you are too much. It's that they weren't enough. Don't let small men make you wish you were a smaller woman. And you are bigger than a blizzard."

My secret hasn't pushed Boone away. In fact, his grip around my hand is more secure.

"Your turn," I manage to breathe out.

"Becca didn't die in a snowstorm. She survived the crash. I found her." Boone sighs heavily.

I gasp. "Here?"

He nods his head. "We were back home for Christmas. She'd secretly bought this cabin for me as an escape. She thought she would surprise me and was driving back from setting up Christmas decorations. She didn't have a lot of experience driving in snowstorms. She wasn't answering her phone. My parents knew where she was, and I went out to find her. I found her alive, but she'd suffered injuries from the crash. They wouldn't let me in the operating room even though I'm a surgeon. They wouldn't let me try to save her."

"What? Why?!" I gasp.

"Protocols," he answers simply.

"Oh, Boone," I whisper, rubbing his hand with my thumb.

"That's why I stopped. If I couldn't save the person I loved, then what was the point of all those years of training?" he mumbles. "So, I moved here. I trashed all the Christmas décor Becca had set up. I thought I was starting over, but really, I was just running away. But God still found me up here. He's been helping me."

"I heard you pray over me last night," I admit, my cheeks burning hot. "I haven't been prayed over since my dad used to do it. He'd tuck me in every night, asking God to protect me and guide me. I'm not sure I've really answered my dad's prayers."

"You heard that?" he asks quietly.

I nod my head. "Thank you."

"The truth is, I haven't always been happy with God," Boone murmurs. "But I've learned God is bigger than our feelings. He must at least have more answers than I do. Maybe not the ones I want, but answers."

"You want to hear something silly I used to pray for when I was little, and I guess I still hope for?" I whisper.

Boone smiles at me. "Yes."

"I used to pray every night after my dad left my room to be married to someone that would sit on a front porch swing with me every day. My parents never sat on our front porch and swung together. I always felt sad for my dad because I'd find him swinging out there by himself, so I'd hop up next to him, and he'd wrap his arm around me, pulling me close. I guess I just wanted that for my dad so much that I decided to pray for it for myself," I detail out. "I know that's silly."

Boone's smile widens. "That's not silly, Kate. I think it's beautiful."

"Do you have a final secret?" I ask Boone, watching as the lights dance in his blue eyes.

"I lied to you yesterday," Boone says, turning his body toward mine. "I still promise that I won't kiss you, but if you kiss me, I'm going to kiss you back."

"Do you want to kiss me?" I question.

"Well, I don't want to not kiss you, Kate." He laughs.

There's something in this moment that has grown warm, our hearts spilling out between one another, not to convince one another that we are perfect, but to convince one another that we are anything but.

"None of what I had to say scared you?" I ask.

"You don't scare me, Kate," Boone says calmly, completely unfazed by all that I've revealed. In fact, he looks more certain than I've seen him. Not that he ever looked uncertain, but this is a different kind of determination.

"I haven't kissed anyone in a long time," I admit. "I'm not sure I'm really that great at it."

Boone laughs. "I believe you told me that you can always right a wrong; it just might come with a lot of effort. I'm okay with some extra effort if that's what it takes."

"Okay, but if I kiss you, it doesn't have to mean anything," I ramble nervously.

"Lying during Santa Secrets?" Boone questions. "Kate, Santa might not bring you the very best gift."

"It's just..." I trail off.

"If you don't want to kiss me, you don't have to kiss me. I just told you that I'm kissing you back." Then Boone scoots closer to me, letting go of my hand to tuck a strand of hair behind my ear before tracing his finger down to my jawline. "Here's the truth, Kate. I like you. I'm not scared of you. In fact, I think you're the perfect amount of enough. I don't know what tomorrow looks like, but I like where we are today."

My breath has halted in my chest. We're wrapped in the scent of pine trees and the closeness of Christmas, as if this moment right now is something we'll never have again. And we won't.

I feel myself leaning toward Boone, closing the gap between us slowly. His hand is still on my face, but he doesn't move toward me. He won't kiss me. It must be me that kisses him. Our faces are only inches apart when I pause and whisper, "When I made you promise that you wouldn't kiss me back, I was hoping you'd break it."

Then my lips are on his lips, and he doesn't hold back. He kisses me fervently, as if I'll never be too much for him.

CHAPTER EIGHTEEN

I wake up smiling, literally. I can feel the way my mouth curves toward my ears.

Boone had tucked me in, prayed over me, and kissed my forehead good night before leaving for the couch for the night. I'd stayed awake for what felt like hours, a thrill zipping through my veins more frenzied than the rush from espresso. It was as if Boone's lips had been made of something stronger than any coffee I'd tasted.

I need to test that theory, though.

The sound of a fire is crackling outside the bedroom door, and it sounds like Boone is in the kitchen, his footsteps gently shuffling along the floorboards. I swing my legs over the bed, standing up to go join him.

I lean on the doorframe when I get to the kitchen, watching him. He's making omelets and is hyperfocused on the task. He's already wearing his standard flannel and jeans, since I assume he's been out to the chicken coop to retrieve fresh eggs for the breakfast he's preparing.

"Merry Christmas," I finally say, announcing my presence, biting on my bottom lip, trying to calm its desire to be on Boone's.

He looks up from the frying pan with a dimpled grin. "I was hoping to surprise you with breakfast in bed. Did I wake you?"

I shake my head, making my way over to him. "No."

He flips the omelet and then turns to face me, putting his arms around my waist, pulling me closer. "Merry Christmas, Kate. Want me to make you a coffee?"

"I was thinking maybe something a little different." Then I lean in and kiss him, feeling my pulse quicken and my heart jump-start for the day as he kisses me back. I pull away. "Theory tested."

"Theory tested?" he questions, his eyebrows arching.

"That kissing you is more energizing than coffee," I answer with a soft smile.

"That is a high compliment coming from you." Boone laughs. "But I'm going to assume you still want that latte."

"You assume correctly," I reply as Boone turns back to the omelet, sliding it onto a plate before handing it to me.

"What do you think?" He looks at me, hopeful.

"I think the student has become the master," I answer.

"Another high compliment," Boone replies smugly, pleased with himself. He walks over to the espresso machine and starts grinding the beans for my latte. "Gingerbread?"

"Yes, please," I answer happily. "So, what are the Christmas plans today?"

"Actually, I have a Christmas present for you, but we kind of have to make it first," Boone says as he moves in a steady rhythm, creating the delicious coffee creations that I'm going to miss when

I return to New York.

"Make it?" I question, taking a bite of the omelet, feeling it soak into my tongue.

"You'll see." The kitchen erupts in a loud sound as he steams the homemade gingerbread creamer before I watch him carefully pour the liquid over the espresso shots in a swirling motion.

Thirty minutes later, Boone bundles me up in his winter gear, telling me it's a surprise, but I have my suspicions when he leads me toward a shed behind the cabin, which I'm guessing is his studio for creating his mugs.

"We're making coffee mugs, aren't we?" I question before we get there, pulling on his hand to stop. "But Boone, I don't even own a coffee machine! I know, that seems impossible coming from someone that is made more of coffee than water, but it's true. I'm one of those impossible people that spends seven dollars every day (okay, more like seventeen dollars every day) on coffee. And I know, I've done the math. It's five hundred dollars a month, which seems insane when you really think about what five hundred dollars can buy, but I prefer living to not, and living equates to five hundred dollars of coffee a month for me."

Boone's lips do that slow crawl into a smile that makes my stomach flop. "Kate, I'm not asking you to defend your spending habits, and use the mugs for tea if you don't use them for coffee."

I scrunch my nose in disgust. "What makes you think I'm even remotely a tea person? Tea is for people who are floating through life, hoping someone else empowered by a stronger beverage makes things happen for them."

"Okay, no tea. Water?" Boone suggests.

"Water mugs? Did you not hear the part where I'm made more of coffee than water?" I question.

Boone steps toward me, dropping my hand to cup my face with his glove. "You know. I really like that you talk so much."

"Are you being sarcastic?" I ask, pressing my lips together.

"No, I'm not. I like that you don't pretend like there's not something on your mind...You just say it," Boone explains. "What's on your mind right now?"

"It's kind of quiet, actually," I tease.

Boone grins. "Oh, is it?"

"No." I laugh. "I'm thinking that I need to order a coffee machine off Amazon so I can use the coffee mugs that you're going to make me, and I kind of hope I get to choose the color, but I also want to know what you want me to have, and that your lips are awfully close to mine, and that you smell like onion from our omelets, and yet I like it even though most people would think it's a repulsive scent in most cases but not really when you want to kiss the person who smells like it, and that I kind of wish last night was every night, that somehow time just stopped with us right here, and what could I do to make that happen, but also is that really what we want, to stay in one moment when we could have a million moments, or if we're even meant to have many more moments, and is this going to be too hard, and are you sure you really like hearing all my thoughts, because now I'm thinking that this could all be a really bad idea because I'm leaving tomorrow and I don't know how to make this work, and now I'm having a hard time breathing because I can feel you moving closer millimeter by millimeter, and..."

Then I can't say anything more because Boone's kissing me, and well, feelings have swallowed up my words.

Boone pulls away, and I wish he were taking my lips with him. "How about we live this moment before we worry about any more?"

I nod my head, slightly dazed.

Boone grabs my hand and leads me to his studio, opening the door and letting me step inside first. It's small but organized. Shelves line an entire wall with beautiful mugs in all colors, some even with engraved designs. There's a pottery wheel, a large metal kiln, a sink, and a workbench. The shed is full, but it's cozy and smells of earthy clay.

"This is amazing, Boone," I say as I walk along the wall of mugs, my finger tracing different handles and rims. I stop when I discover a mug with a chicken stamped into its side. "Is this Goose?"

Boone laughs. "Goose and I aren't that close, you know."

I point to the gash above my eye that's been healing up nicely, thanks to Boone's herbal concoctions. "Really?"

"You just caught her on a bad day," Boone defends. "That, and she doesn't really see a lot of other people."

I roll my eyes. "You believe what you want to. I think she hates me, and when she finds out you stole her chicken coop lights for me, her hatred might turn to vengeance. With that being said, I do not want a chicken on my mug."

Boone grins. "Noted."

As I continue to look around his studio, Boone prepares the wheel.

"Do you ship a lot of mugs?" I question.

"Enough," Boone replies.

"What's enough?" I ask.

"Some months a hundred, some months more," he answers. "Now, are you ready?"

I look over at him, and he's prepared two small stools, one closer to the pottery wheel and the other one directly behind it. I shrug my shoulders. "I'm always up for a challenge."

I sit down on the stool closest to the wheel, slightly intimidated by what's in front of me, if I'm completely honest. I took ceramics in college one semester, and when I say 'I took ceramics', I mean I went to two classes until I transferred out of it. Art wasn't new to me. I'd painted the typical apple in a bowl and had done some abstract art, which was so abstract to me that I didn't know what I was doing, but my art teacher informed me I was a genius. I'm still not sure what she saw in me; however, I was thankful for the passing grade.

But ceramics. There was a different rhythm to it, and I had two left feet or, I guess, two left hands.

Boone had already moistened the wheel, and it was spinning, a lump of clay flattened to the wheel to secure it. And that's about the extent of my knowledge of a potter's wheel and how to get started.

I feel Boone sitting behind me, the firm warmth of his chest against my back.

"I might mess this all up," I mumble.

Boone laughs, and I can feel his breath on my neck, sending a flickering breeze of goosebumps down my spine. "Messes happen, Kate. I still make them occasionally, but I promise I'm here to make sure we make something beautiful together."

I lean back against him. "Are we still talking about mugs?"

I can feel his smile without seeing it in the way his chest softens. Then his mouth finds my jawline, making me sigh before he murmurs, "I could talk about other beautiful things."

"But then I won't have a mug to drink the coffee I'm going to make myself when I order that coffee machine off Amazon," I insist. "And if I don't have a mug that we made together when I drink my coffee, how will I remember you?"

"I'm pretty sure the part where I saved your life will help jog your memory of me," Boone says as he smiles against the side of my head.

"Well, I guess there's that," I tease.

"But let's make this mug. Okay," he says gently as he grabs my hands with his, leading them toward the clay. "When clay isn't centered, it wobbles. Sometimes you must recenter repeatedly until you get it. Kind of like life."

I smile at his hands over mine.

The clay feels cold and smooth beneath my hands. His hands move expertly, guiding mine as we push the clay into what appears to be a cone at first. His thumbs push into mine, pushing into the clay. I'm mesmerized by the movement, by the feel of watching the clay turn into something different, something new. Boone adds water as we need it, making sure the clay remains moldable. His breath has been steady against my neck as he concentrates on moving my hands as the clay turns from a cone to a cup.

"This would be easier if you were just doing it yourself, wouldn't it?" I ask quietly.

"Easier? Yes. But then I wouldn't get to have my arms wrapped around you, sharing this moment," he answers without any hesitation. "I like my arms around you."

I swallow down my honesty in this moment, trying to breathe in what's happening right now and not what will happen later. Me leaving Boone and not knowing if it's going to mean for a little while or forever.

Chapter Nineteen

The mug is formed and drying. Boone let me pick out the glaze, a blue as soft and bright as his eyes. He said he'd mail me the mug when it was finished. Time seems to be moving too fast now as the reminder for my flight in the morning dings on my phone.

"Boone." I sigh as I lean into him. We're sitting on the couch, sipping on a shared latte, my back nuzzled into his chest and my legs pulled up to my knees.

"Yes?" he asks, his fingers lightly combing through my hair.

"I'm trying really hard to just enjoy the moment, but I can't help but think about what's next," I admit. "I mean, let's be honest with each other. We're adults. We have very real, very lived-in lives apart from each other. We don't really make sense. What if all of this was just meant to be for now and not for longer?"

I feel Boone stiffen slightly, almost unnoticeably, but my nerves are on high alert and picking up on any subtle differences. "What do you want, Kate?"

"It's not as simple as what I want," I ramble as I turn to face him. "It's what we both want, or don't want, or might not want any longer down the road."

"Kate, I think you're just scared." Boone sighs.

"Scared of what?" I question.

"Scared that you'll fall in love with me and I won't fall in love with you," he says plainly, a pain point from Santa Secrets the night before.

My jaw drops slightly. "That's not fair."

"Life's not fair, Kate, but just because it's not fair, doesn't mean that you don't try," Boone argues, without raising his voice. In fact, he's completely calm and collected, even going so far as to take a sip of coffee.

"Aren't you scared?" I ask, because I can't be the only one between us trying to sort out how this would even work and how it would feel if it didn't. If we tried and we failed.

Boone sighs. "When I came to this cabin, I was hurt...suffering. I was scared then. I hid from feeling anything else because I thought I had felt too much. Hiding kept me safe, but I also began to realize that it kept me from living, that I needed to feel again. And then I found you. What were the chances I'd find a woman in a blizzard at Christmas on the same road as I'd found Becca, but that this time I was able to save her? I think I was meant to find you, Kate."

"But what if we just don't work, Boone?" I ask.

"But what if we do, Kate?" he questions back.

I open my mouth to say something, but there's a sound I haven't heard for days—a car door closing. My eyes quickly flicker to the window by the door before the door swings wide open.

"Merry Christmas!" a woman exclaims loudly, her hands overflowing with food. Her hair is dark and cascading in large curls around her face, and if she were about a foot taller, she might look like Boone.

Then a tall man with graying facial hair follows her in with my luggage. "We bring food and something that I'm guessing a woman named Kate is very much missing."

I hop up from the couch, hurrying to my long-lost bag full of clothes that fit. "You are a Christmas angel!"

"Pretty sure that's you, dear," the woman laughs. "I'm Boone's mom, Elizabeth, but you can call me Liz. This is Kurt, Boone's dad and the love of my life."

I smile at the introduction. "You're the banana-bread queen."

Her entire face lights up. "That's me. I'm sorry we couldn't get up here sooner to bring food. When Boone called and told me what happened, I immediately began trying to remember what was up here, and I was afraid you'd both starve."

Boone stands up from the couch, striding toward his mom with open arms, wrapping them around her when he reaches her. "We didn't starve. Kate is a great chef and teacher. She even taught me how to make an omelet."

Liz's eyes widen as she looks at me. "And it was edible?"

I nod my head, laughing. "Yes, very edible. Amazing, actually."

"Let me help you with all of this," Boone says to his mom as he grabs bags and dishes that she's holding onto.

Then Liz's mouth hangs wide open, and I follow the direction in which she is staring—the Christmas tree. "What's this?"

"A Christmas tree," Boone replies plainly.

"What is a Christmas tree doing in your cabin?" Liz questions, a thread of hope looped through her words.

"I didn't want Kate to miss out on Christmas just because she was stuck with me," Boone answers.

"He used the chicken coop lights," I add, grinning.

Liz looks over at me. "Well, Kate, I wish he would have found you sooner. It's about time there was good cooking and Christmas in this place."

And I know she doesn't mean anything permanent with her comment, but there's something about it that causes my pulse to quicken. The Christmas snow globe Boone and I had been stuck in is no longer. Life outside the glass has entered, and Boone's real life has resumed.

It is only hours until mine does, too.

I pick up my luggage and then turn to Kurt. "How did you find this?"

"Small-town perks," Kurt replies. "Your rental is at our house, too. Somehow, mostly unscathed, all things considered."

"Wow, thank you. I was really worried about Miranda, but I told myself she was made of steel or aluminum or whatever Mitsubishi Mirages are made of, and that she'd be fine. She really didn't want to make the trek, you know. I wasn't quite sure how I'd be able to get her back." I ramble until I realize everyone is staring at me—Boone with amusement, his parents with curiosity.

"You named the car Miranda?" Liz finally asks.

I bite my lower lip. "Well, I figured naming the car I decided needed to be my trusty steed through the snow was not just a necessity, but an admirable thing to do. Turns out, she wasn't so trusty, or maybe it was the driver, but either way, thank goodness Boone found us."

Boone's grin has doubled in size as my words have grown.

Finally, Liz laughs and replies, "Oh, I like you. You're fun. I can see why Boone cut you down a tree."

I feel my cheeks warm. "Well, I'm going to go change into something that fits. Thanks again for retrieving this for me."

Then I quickly leave the room, shutting Boone's bedroom door behind me before leaning on it, sighing.

I hadn't thought I'd meet Boone's parents. Not now, possibly not ever. Of course, I'd thought about it. My mind had begun to wander off into unknown territory, a place I kept barricaded because it was a place I'd been to before in my ignorance with a boyfriend I'd managed to keep for five months. Planning a life with someone only to have the fantasy ripped away the moment they decided it wasn't going to work, which was the polite way to say, 'It's definitely you.'

I am more of a woman of the hour than a woman for a lifetime, or at least that's what my track record from the last twenty-two years of boyfriends, and lack of them, has concluded.

Boone is weak. Maybe he doesn't realize it, and I'm not sure I realized it at first either. I thought I was the weaker one, but I'm the first woman he's allowed into his life since Becca, and he didn't exactly allow it. I kind of managed to force my way in through my own reckless decisions.

I'm fun now because I'm new and different and maybe even

exciting. But he'll realize sooner or later that I am just the woman that helped him feel again, and not the one he wants forever.

I need to be the stronger one of us right now.

I lift my suitcase onto Boone's bed, unzipping it, thankful to see things that are mine. I rub my hand over the familiar fabrics. I choose a festive red turtleneck sweater and black leather pants that I don't have to roll around my waist to fit. Then I internally squeal when I pull out my makeup bag and quickly snatch up my mascara, running to the bathroom attached to Boone's bedroom.

"Better," I say to myself in the mirror.

I return to the bedroom, packing my bag back up and folding Boone's clothes neatly on his bed. I've made my decision, and I stiffen my spine with resolve before I take a breath and go back out to ask Boone's parents for a ride back to Miranda so I can get myself back to the airport and resume my real life, and Boone can go choose the woman he wants to find a new forever with and not just be stuck with me.

CHAPTER TWENTY

"Kate, you know this isn't about me. This is about you," Boone argues.

We're outside, me, bundled up in my flimsy pink coat and stilettos, and him, unprepared for this Christmas chaos I've decided to create. For his own good, of course. He doesn't know me. Not really. He just knows enough to find me interesting. For now.

I always seem intriguing at first. Something you take a longer look at and then quickly look away from when you discover the magic is just a mess.

"We just met, Boone. This was fun, and I really appreciate you rescuing me. I do. I owe you my life," I reply with a settled sigh. I've made up my mind. There's no going back now.

Boone grabs for my hands, but I'm too quick, my reflexes ready to protect me from his warmth and pleading, and I tuck my hands within my arms as I cross them.

"Kate. You're scared. That's all this is."

"I'm not scared," I defend. "I'm just being honest. We barely know each other, and we got swept up in Christmas. You didn't choose me, and I didn't choose you. This just was what it was, and

I need to get back to my life, so you can get back to yours."

"Kate." Boone utters my name as I study his face. I've always been one to face a challenge straight on. The way his face wrinkles isn't with anger or even frustration, which I've seen many times; it's something different. Something softer. "Did you not feel something?"

I sigh. "Feeling something isn't the same as facts. We aren't made for each other. I'm just the first woman that caused you to feel something since Becca. Some irrational, ridiculous, well-dressed stranger that you'll forget about as soon as you find someone new. Someone who fits your life better than I do."

Boone's chest falls. He steps closer to me, and I'm afraid he's going to go all in. Try to make me stay when I know I need to go. But he doesn't. He opens the back door to his parents' Jeep. "I'm not going to argue with you, Kate. I'll fight for you, but I'm not going to fight against you. You're doing enough of that yourself."

I blink, my jaw dropping slightly before I snatch it back up. I expected him to argue with me. Everyone always does. My tongue is twitching, expecting words to roll off it, but I have none. Kate Everett is officially silent, and I don't know how to proceed, so I just get in the Jeep, Boone still holding the door.

Before he closes it, he looks at me with what appears to be admiration glittering in his blue eyes. "And you're not some irrational, ridiculous woman, Kate. I hope one day you'll let someone in, so they can really know how remarkable you are."

But Boone doesn't understand what knowing me really means. No one ever has loved me when they've really *known* me. My imperfections are just as big and loud as the parts that make me shimmer. What makes me great also always makes me not great enough.

It's weird how you can be both too much and not enough, and yet, that was me. Too loud meant not quiet enough. Too confident meant not humble enough. Too bold meant not modest enough. Too much was always not enough of something.

Then the door shuts, and my emotions begin to swirl within me, like the blizzard that brought me to Boone.

CHAPTER
TWENTY-ONE

"K ate?"

I'm looking at my phone screen, which happens to be displaying my Amazon cart with a Nespresso machine. I delete it, and even though it disappears, my hope that the mug Boone and I made together arrives at my apartment doesn't. I don't know if he'll still send it, but I have a feeling he will. Boone is as bitter as his coffee, which means, he's not.

"What's up?" I ask my boss who doesn't really act like my boss. Stephanie acts more like a supervisor who doesn't care what I do because she knows I don't just always get the job done; I get it done better than anyone else does.

"Is there a reason you've logged fifty hours in four days?" she questions.

I shrug my shoulders as Stephanie's glasses hug into her forehead as she raises her eyebrows. "Getting a jump start on some of the new year marketing campaigns. I know our clients will appreciate some solid marketing after the holiday season."

"I'm sure they will but, Kate, I can't have you log eighty hours this week, and that's where you're headed at this rate. Why don't you take the rest of the day off?" she suggests.

"I'm leaving tomorrow for Tulsa," I remind her. "I need to finish a few things up, and I'll be gone for a few days."

"Or how about a few weeks?" she suggests. "You know I love what you accomplish but, Kate, I'd be a horrible boss if I only cared about you doing a great job at your work."

"I'm fine, Stephanie," I reply.

Her eyebrows arch. "You're fine? Kate, I've seen you not once, but twice, chug the entire pot of coffee in the break room. Which, I know you love coffee, but even this has seemed quite extreme."

It was disgusting, too. Both times. The coffee tasted like dirt, but coffee is my comfort, and I guess I've needed a lot of that since getting back to New York—even if it felt like an uncomfortable hug from an ex-boyfriend with how acidic the brew had been.

"Kate, what exactly happened over Christmas?" she finally asks.

I've kept silent about Boone, except to Kevin. Kevin has heard it all, and my last few texts he'd read but hadn't responded to.

I tried to help it, but I blame the social media algorithms, really.

I'd been scrolling Facebook when an ad for a chicken coop had popped up. I immediately took a screen shot and sent it to Kevin. Then he called me.

"Kate, why are you sending me this?" he'd said.

"It looked nice," I replied quickly, immediately regretting how quick my fingers could fly on my phone screen.

"Does this have anything to do with Boone?" he had questioned.

"No!"

And even I knew my answer was too emphatic, too loud, too much of a lie.

It had most definitely been because of Boone. The chicken coop was nice but not as cozy as the one Boone had made his hens, and I hated that I knew that. That he cared that much. That he'd lit up their coop with so much love and then taken those lights and strung them around a Christmas tree just for me.

Another time, Facebook had obviously crawled into my subconscious and decided to take me directly to Boone's online mug store through an ad, which then led to me losing hours of sleep as I looked at every listing. And then I may or may not have decided that was the opportune time to Google him.

I felt the Internet had become a sort of ghost of Christmas past, except it was Boone's and not mine. Past articles about an award he'd won in California as a surgeon, about Becca's car accident, and even one about how he graduated top of his class—his future bright and shiny.

And then, just like I'd been transported to his past, my un-caffeinated brain had decided to step into the role of Christmas future, but not the desolate future where I ended up alone—no, it had decided to have me marry Boone. To torture me with how it could have been great.

It doesn't help that I'd accidentally stolen a pair of Boone's wool socks and I'm wearing them every night. Wearing them feels like I am being swallowed whole by his warmth. And I miss his warmth.

That's why I was chugging coffee at work, trying to keep myself from doing irrational things, like friending Boone on Facebook or placing a massive handmade mug order.

Except uncaffeinated or caffeinated, all I could do was think about Boone. Although, at least caffeinated, I could get a few things done.

"I met someone." I sigh.

Stephanie's red lips spread in a smile. "Kate Everett met someone?"

I nod my head.

"Then why are you here?" she asks, putting her hands on her hips.

"Because I just don't think it'll work."

"If you put half the effort into a relationship that you do into your career, I guarantee you that it will," Stephanie says. "Besides, it's not like you can really have a happily ever after with your computer."

And while Stephanie might be right, my computer always chooses me back. It won't leave. It won't think I'm too much. It won't tell me that it's changed its mind when I've been typing on it for too long.

"I'll finish this up and then head out. See you next year," I say to Stephanie.

She concedes, knowing that I'll always argue my way to the very end of a conversation until I win. "Okay, Kate."

Stephanie walks out of my office as my phone buzzes.

It's a photo from my brother.

I open the file, and my eyes instantly pool with tears.

It's a framed photo of me with my dad. I'm around thirteen, wearing a sweater that my dad had made for me. He took a knitting class for an entire year, secretly, so he could make it for me. It had an armadillo on it. I'd never received something so special. In the photo my dad has his arm around me, leaning down on my head as my frizzy hair tickled at his face.

With the photo, my brother typed out, *I found this photo and had it framed for your Christmas gift this year. I know we're celebrating tomorrow night, but Kate—just because Dad is gone doesn't mean that there isn't someone else that won't love you as much as he did. Your armadillo shell has protected you from so much, but I'm worried that you've also allowed it to keep you from just as much. Not everyone is a predator, except maybe Goose, at least from your version of her. I love you.*

I laugh through my tears at the mention of Goose. She's most definitely a predator.

I look at my dad's face, a sense of awe and wonder radiating from his smile.

"I wish you could tell me what to do, Dad," I whisper. "I just want to make you proud."

CHAPTER
TWENTY-TWO

I didn't sleep that night.

As my veins slowly lost their steady supply of espresso, my mind had no choice but to think about Boone irrationally. I'd pulled up our silly selfie on my phone, staring at him like I was staring at a shooting star.

And I am completely aware how ridiculous that sounds.

I miss him.

I hate it.

But I do.

I miss his smile, the way it slowly tiptoes across his cheeks until he's smiling as if he has a special smile that's just for me.

I miss the feeling of his hand wrapped around mine.

I miss the way he isn't afraid to be honest back—to surrender his thoughts to my own.

And I miss his gingerbread latte.

"I need coffee," I say to myself, looking at the clock on my phone. I still have two hours until I need to be at the airport to fly to Tulsa to spend New Year's with my brother, Maisy Jo, and the kids.

I snatch up my purse from the small glass table in my foyer before pulling my coat around me and rushing toward the door. In boots, not stilettos. I am not going to get on a plane in shoes that aren't sensible ever again. But I pause before I can turn the doorknob.

I don't want to trek down to another disappointing coffee shop where their beans aren't as bold, and their creamers aren't as home-made, and their baristas aren't Boone.

Boone ruined coffee for me.

And if I don't have coffee, what do I really have?

I know that's teeter-tottering on the edge of insanity, but also, I'd done crazy things for the love of coffee. I'd almost died, after all. But almost dying had brought me to Boone.

And if I am really pinch-my-cheeks-hard honest with myself, Boone was right.

For thirty-seven years, it's been me against the world. I've always told myself that I'm not afraid of a challenge, but really, when I dig deep within, I'm just not afraid of the things that don't matter the most. I'm terrified of the things that do.

Boone had seen it. He'd seen that I was scared.

And the strange thing is—*he* isn't scared by it.

In fact, he really hadn't been scared of any part of me, just like my dad was never scared of me, either. Just like how my dad, instead, was in awe of it.

Maybe, just maybe, Boone is a big enough man to love every part of me—the too muchness and the not enoughs. But I'd run away.

It wasn't Boone that had left me, or pushed me, or even tried to convince me to stay. He'd just let me be me, because he wasn't against me. He was Team Kate, and I'd quit. On Christmas, no less. I guess that makes me the Scrooge.

My eyes widen, my pulse quickens, and my toes dance in Boone's wool socks.

"What in the world am I doing?!" I lecture myself. "Kate Everett is a lot of things, but she's not a quitter."

I pull out my phone, checking flights to Denver. There's one flying out in two hours. Within minutes, I have a ticket. Then I push down on my brother's name.

He answers on the second ring, "Hey, Katydilla. Headed to the airport?"

"Almost, but Kev, I'm so sorry to do this. I'm not coming to Oklahoma," I say quickly as I rush to grab random pieces of clothes, throwing them in my suitcase. "I have somewhere else I need to be."

I can practically hear my brother's lips widen in a smile through the phone. "Atta girl, Kate."

"I haven't even told you where I'm going." I laugh.

"When all this works out, there's a property going up for sale a couple miles from us. You and Boone should move here," Kevin says.

"Kev, I don't even know if this is going to work out."

"Well, when it does, Maisy Jo and I could use some babysitters," he teases.

"You haven't even met the guy," I argue.

"Any guy that's able to make Katydilla shrug off her shell isn't going to be that easy to get rid of. I was worried for a minute. You almost did your famous tuck and roll..."

I interrupt him. "My famous tuck and roll?"

"Like an armadillo, Kate. You're the one that was obsessed with them. When they fear getting hurt, they roll up in a ball to protect the most vulnerable parts of themselves and roll away," he quickly explains.

Rolling away. Running away. It's all the same thing.

But this time I'm not going to do it.

I'm going to run toward something that matters most.

Well, fly toward, and then get into a rental car that is definitely not a shoebox on wheels like Miranda had been.

CHAPTER
TWENTY-THREE

B oone's cabin looks smaller as I pull up into the drive, this time in a truck with four-wheel drive and chains. I don't exactly know what chains do, but I'd demanded the best at the Avis counter, and they must have had a detailed report of my incident with Miranda from a week ago, because they also made me take out insurance.

The sound of the truck's engine announces my arrival before I can, and the Boone I'd been staring at on my phone screen all week is now on his porch, flesh and beard. The Boone that told me he wasn't scared of me, that he could essentially handle my ups and downs, my too much and not enough. Now he's leaning up against the doorframe, his arms crossed, watching me.

I open the truck door, my boots finding balance on the ground before my brain does, causing me to just stand there like a moron with no words to say when I know I need to be the one that has all the words to say.

"This isn't Oklahoma, you know," Boone finally says, breaking the silence between us.

The left side of my mouth curves up in a half smile. "Must have taken a wrong turn."

"What are you doing here, Kate?" Boone asks, not moving.

"I heard the world's best latte was made here," I tease. "And well, this man I met last week ruined coffee for me. Ruined a lot of things, actually."

"Sounds like you should run away from that guy."

I start walking toward Boone, my boots a much better match for the snow than my stilettos. "Well, you see, I did. But then I realized that maybe the things I've been running away from are actually the things I should be running toward."

Boone pushes off the doorframe, taking a step in my direction. "I'm listening..."

"All my life it's been me against the world. I've fought hard. I'm pretty stubborn, you know," I say, taking another step forward.

Boone grins at this. "I do know."

"But then this man said something. He said he'd fight for me, that he wouldn't fight against me," I continue.

"Sounds like a great guy," Boone interjects.

"Oh, just wait, he gets better." I smile, closing the gap between us until we're so close I can feel Boone's warmth radiating off him. "He also said I was fighting myself, and I realized, after many, many terrible cups of coffee, that he was right. And you see, I have this thing about being wrong."

Boone's hand finds mine, and then he prompts gently, "Remind me."

"I don't mind being wrong, but I can't stand staying wrong when there's a way to figure out what's right. And when I'm really honest with myself, being with you feels right even though I'm scared. I don't think I'm the kind that's easy to love."

His finger traces my jawline, lifting my chin so my eyes look into his blue ones. "Kate, I think you're a lot easier to love than you think. You just have to let someone try."

My teeth sink into my bottom lip. "Boone, do you want to try?"

Boone pulls at my hand, leading me toward the cabin before stopping short of the porch. The porch that now has a swing. "I want someone to sit with on the porch swing, too, Kate."

My porch swing Santa Secret.

Although it was a prayer I prayed when I was just a kid, it's always been something I've wanted. To grow old with someone that wanted to grow old with me, that wanted to sit and reminisce on the old memories while hoping for the new together. And I think my dad would want that for me, too.

Tears well up in my eyes. "You built me a swing?"

"I know you don't want to be here at the cabin. I'll build you a porch swing wherever you are, Kate, because it's not really about the porch swing. It's about who is sitting in the swing with you."

His hands are now on my waist, pulling me closer to him until there is no air between us. It's just him, me, and my weak knees.

"Okay," I whisper into the fog of our feelings and breath. "But Boone, you have to promise me something."

I look up, my mind tracing his lips curving into a smile until my eyes reach his.

"Anything," he breathes.

"You must promise to keep me in coffee, because you really did completely, forever ruin me on every other coffee creamer out there. Not even the coffee creamer from that fancy coffee shop in New York was good enough. It's all terrible. Necessary, but terrible, and I accidentally stole a pair of your wool socks, and I'm not giving them back. In fact, I would like six more pairs so I can have a pair for every day of the week, and I really need to apologize to your parents, because I'm sure they think I'm a terrible person for how I left you on Christmas, and..."

But there are no more *and*s because Boone's lips are on mine, hushing my rambling with a kiss that's as strong as it is soft. When he pulls away, he smiles. "I can make good on that promise right now."

"Thank goodness," I reply. "Because while I did mainly come here for you, I was also really excited about a gingerbread latte."

EPILOGUE

Three years later...

It isn't Kate Everett against the world anymore. It is Boone and Kate Montgomery, creating their own world together.

Two years ago, Kevin walked me down the aisle in the church where Boone's parents were married. It was simple, perfect, and all our guests received handmade mugs with a chicken kissing an armadillo stamped on them. My mother came. She gave us a crystal gravy boat. It holds coffee creamer in our refrigerator.

Our refrigerator that isn't in the cabin in the woods or in an apartment in New York.

Our refrigerator and porch swing reside in Oklahoma on our five-acre homestead, two miles down the road from Kevin, Maisy Jo, and the kids. Goose lives here, too. She still hates me, but jokes on her, because I married her rooster.

It wasn't hard giving up my job in the city. I thought it would be, but it turns out being married to a person is a lot more fun than being married to a career. I do a lot of freelance marketing now for small businesses, including Boone's coffee mugs, which now has a larger shed, a larger kiln, and a larger customer base.

We still own the cabin. Boone said we could sell it, but I didn't want him to lose that piece of his past. There's a difference between holding onto something that holds you back and holding onto something that means something to you. We visit at least twice a year and hope we get snowed in.

A steaming latte appears from behind me as I'm looking out the window at the winter wonderland our little homestead became overnight. It's in my favorite mug. The soft blue one that reflects mountain skies and Boone's eyes.

"Thank you," I murmur as I take a sip. Gingerbread. My favorite.

"How are my lovely ladies this morning?" Boone croons as he bends down and kisses my ever-growing belly. I find a new stretch mark every day.

"We don't know that it's a girl," I remind him. We'd had the sonogram months ago, and I'd refused to allow the young woman to tell us.

"I know," Boone says as he stands back up and places a soft kiss on my forehead. "But I wouldn't mind a mini Katydilla."

"She'd be a force." I laugh.

"That's what I'm counting on." Boone smiles as he wraps his arms around me from behind, joining me in watching the world outside our window.

Not every moment is as perfect as this one right now, but Boone has helped me enjoy moments as they come instead of worrying about running out of them. So, we take each moment at a time, savoring them and making sure we don't miss something that one day we'll realize was everything.

Then I feel something new, something sharp and yet exciting.

"Boone," I gasp.

"What?" He steps around to face me, his eyes wide.

My lips slowly curve into a soft, knowing grin. "It's time."

His hands find my belly, gently caressing it. "It's time?!"

I nod my head. "Time to make a memory."

ACKNOWLEDGEMENTS

Prior to this publication, all my previous works have lacked a team beyond my own family and friends. While, I am still incredibly grateful for the support I have in them (*you all know who you are!*), it's been such a joy to find others that are excited about this story and my writing.

I'd like to give a few quick *thank you's* to a few people who made putting this story together an absolute delight.

First, Jessica Flory. I don't think you know how much I truly appreciate your enthusiasm when it comes to my writing. You were quick to help, but also quick to celebrate as you read through to help develop this story into what it is. If not for you, Kate wouldn't have had the character arc that she did that really rounded out what she needed to accomplish. Thank you for loving my characters almost as much as I do!

Kristyn Fortner, I'm not the only one thankful for you. My mom is, too! Up to this point, she's been the only one helping me through grammatical edits. Thank you for squeezing me into your schedule and helping this story become polished. You really helped make the words shine!

Rachel Parker! Thank you so much for bringing Kate and

Boone together in the character art. Not only that, but thank you for being the light that you are in the closed door romance community. You truly help so many people by connecting readers to authors, and authors to readers.

To my ARC readers...THANK YOU! I truly appreciate how excited you were to get snowed in with Kate and Boone and inspire others to get snowed in, too.

Thank you to *Messenger Coffee* out of Kansas City. I know you have no idea why you are being thanked, but I consumed pounds of your espresso beans during this writing process. For that matter, I need to also thank my milk cow, Pumpkin. She produced all the creamy milk needed for those one-thousand-and-one lattes. Maybe one-thousand-and-two. I lost count.

Thank you to my husband, Justin. You always take all my too muchness and not enoughs, and determine that I'm just right for you. You give me space to grow, to learn, to become, and to pursue writing. I wouldn't know how to write a MMC that knows how to love so selflessly if it was not for you.

To my kids, I pray every day for your future spouses and that they make you feel like you're *just right*, just like your dad makes me feel.

All gratitude and glory to Jesus, for without Him, I would not know any of this life I do.

This has been a blizzard of a short season putting this story together, and instead of, *It Could Have Been Great*, is truly has been.

ABOUT THE AUTHOR

 Shelbey Kendall is a storyteller at heart, with a deep love for Jesus and family. She's a Kansas native that loves wide-open spaces and pink skies. When she's not writing, you'll find her savoring a fourth cup of coffee while homeschooling her three children, and probably cooking something with potatoes.

As the creator of *The Sonshine Sister Club* series for young girls, Shelbey has shared her passion for creating relatable characters that show no matter how imperfect we are, our imperfections do not keep us from a perfect Jesus. Now, she's bringing that same heart to one of her favorite genres with her debut romance novella, *It Could Have Been Great.*

She loves connecting with her readers and would love for you to follow along as she creates more stories that braid heart and humor together.

IG: @shelbeykendallauthor
www.shelbeykendall.com

Made in the USA
Middletown, DE
06 January 2026

26688082R00102